A WEEK IN THE LIFE OF A GRECO-ROMAN WOMAN

HOLLY BEERS

ivp
Academic
An imprint of InterVarsity Press
Downers Grove, Illinois

InterVarsity Press
P.O. Box 1400, Downers Grove, IL 60515-1426
ivpress.com
email@ivpress.com

InterVarsity Press® is the book-publishing division of InterVarsity Christian Fellowship/USA®, a
movement of students and faculty active on campus at hundreds of universities, colleges, and
schools of nursing in the United States of America, and a member movement of the International
Fellowship of Evangelical Students. For information about local and regional activities, visit
intervarsity.org.

Cover design: Cindy Kiple
Interior design: Beth McGill
Images: ancient Carthage mosaic: © EnginKorkmaz / iStock / Getty Images Plus

ISBN 978-0-8308-2484-7 (print)
ISBN 978-0-8308-4989-5 (digital)

Library of Congress Cataloging-in-Publication Data
A catalog record for this book is available from the Library of Congress.

P 22 21 20 19 18 17 16 15 14 13 12 11 10 9 8 7 6 5 4 3
Y 39 38 37 36 35 34 33 32 31 30 29 28 27 26 25 24 23 22

"Trying to imagine what life would have been like in the Roman empire can be hard enough, it can be harder too if you are trying to imagine what life was like for women, whose voices are mostly muted and marginalized in the annals of history. So it is quite rewarding to have someone like Dr. Holly Beers do the hard work of research and creative storytelling to help us imagine the life of women in the Greco-Roman world."

Michael F. Bird, academic dean and lecturer in theology at Ridley College in Melbourne, Australia

"From the opening pages, I could not put down her story. Beers takes her extensive knowledge of the New Testament and shapes a fictional woman's journey of discovery of the gospel and the early church community. The fast-paced narrative is filled with dialogue as biblical characters—Paul, Priscilla, Timothy, and others—come to life under Beers's skilled storytelling. This is a must-read for men and women of all ages who want a fresh look at the power and promise of the gospel."

Lynn H. Cohick, provost/dean of Denver Seminary

"Holly Beers does some important things in this enjoyable work of historical fiction. First, she makes me care about the characters at the center of the drama. Second, she provides an accessible introduction to the religious, economic, and social world of a Greco-Roman woman with all its difficulties and complexities. Finally, she demonstrates the ways in which those worlds would be upset and transformed through an encounter with the burgeoning Christian community. It's a great resource for anyone wanting to know about the experiences of women in the first years of the church's life."

Esau McCaulley, assistant professor of New Testament at Wheaton College, coordinator of Call and Response Ministries

"This week-long snapshot of a life offers a truly intersectional approach to a woman's experience, which allows the reader to get an informed feel for how gender, economic status, cultural customs, gynecological health, technology, family structures, and religious practices might coalesce. Re-embedding Paul's proclamation of Christ within this fictional—but potentially realistic and certainly based on careful research—context enables modern readers to hear anew both the scandal and the hope that the gospel must have held for its earliest hearers."

Kara Lyons-Pardue, professor of New Testament, Point Loma Nazarene University

"Caught between her fidelity to Artemis, fascination with Jesus, and fear of reprisal, Anthia and her readers experience the gravity of her dilemma: Will she risk everything to follow Jesus? I highly recommend this book, not only as a gripping page-turner but also as a powerful exegetical tool—rich with historical and cultural details that bring the Bible to life through the eyes of a first-century woman."

Alicia R. Jackson, assistant professor of Old Testament, Vanguard University

"From the sounds in the public and private spaces to the smells of ancient bread and fish, readers will find themselves learning about the ancient world while immersed in a compelling story about a woman, her community, and her journey of faith. Whether for personal reading or as a course textbook, Holly Beers's story will leave a lasting impression on every reader!"

Beth M. Stovell, associate professor of Old Testament, Ambrose University, National Catalyst for Theological and Spiritual Formation for Vineyard Canada

"*A Week in the Life of a Greco-Roman Woman* gives us beautifully vivid storytelling and superb treatment of the historical background. Each element breathes life to the other such that the story is richer and the historical background more vibrant because of the book's unique genre."

Rebekah Josberger, professor of Hebrew and Old Testament at Multnomah Biblical Seminary

"This book brims with information about life in Ephesus in the first century and shines a light on the experience of people in the Greco-Roman world and how they might have engaged the early church. Beers is a great storyteller and the book is hard to put down. I recommend it for anyone wanting to get a feel for first-century life as it was lived on the ground."

Jeannine Brown, professor of New Testament and director of online programs at Bethel Seminary, San Diego and St. Paul

"*A Week in the Life of a Greco-Roman Woman* is a fantastic way to engage any student of the Bible with the real people, real places, and real challenges of the first-century church. . . . Not only do we walk away with an all-too-rare woman's lens on the impact of the Gospel on her world, we are left with a deeply personal testimony of the confrontation of Artemis's city with the Way of Jesus."

Sandra Richter, Robert H. Gundry Chair of Biblical Studies, Westmont College

"Combining a winsome story of Anthia, a poor Ephesian woman, with informative historical sidebars, Beers offers modern readers a memorable glimpse of first-century life and the early Christian mission."

Laura C. Sweat Holmes, associate professor of New Testament and associate dean of graduate studies, Seattle Pacific Seminary

"Holly Beers has written a creative and engaging story of life in first-century Ephesus that presents background information helpful to understanding the New Testament material of that provenance. The plot line of her story suggests a way of understanding 1 Timothy 2:15 in its historical setting that all readers of the New Testament should consider. An educational and thought-provoking read!"

Karen H. Jobes, Gerald F. Hawthorne Professor Emerita of New Testament Greek and Exegesis, Wheaton College and Graduate School

For my parents, Jerry and Phyllis,
*who have modeled a lifelong love for the Bible,
and my sister Kelly, who cares deeply about
the experience of women and mothers
both in the ancient world and today.*

And for my two church small groups:
*our Monday night family group (Tori, Andy,
Cody, Robb, Kacy, Brian, and kids), our primary
Jesus-family in Santa Barbara for the past six
years, who have welcomed my historical-cultural
comments and given me space to ponder big
theological questions, and my Wednesday
morning women's group (Kerry, Amber, Patti,
Amy, and Ally), whose passion for women
in the Bible makes me feel at home.*

CONTENTS

Acknowledgments

This book would not have been possible without the time and space given to me by my husband, Max, and our three young children, Noah, Moses, and Eden. Thank you for understanding, in your own ways, my love for the Bible and need to tell this story.

PROLOGUE

Anthia held her breath. She was nervous. Dorema's labor was not progressing well, and Anthia could see from her friend's bloodshot eyes and blank stare that she was exhausted from pushing.

Making a conscious effort to breathe normally, Anthia patted Dorema's arm and told her that all was well. Dorema needed to believe it so that she could manage her contractions and push. Anthia stood at Dorema's back, where she was supporting her friend's body on the birthing stool. The midwife pulled out a small metal mirror and placed it between Dorema's legs. "See, Dorema! The baby's head is here! Look!"

Figure P.1. A midwife assists a woman who has recently given birth

Dorema strained to look, and as Anthia moved to assist her she caught a glimpse of herself in the polished metal of the mirror. Her dark hair was parted, as always, in the middle and pulled back into a knot at the back of her head. Her brown eyes were pinched in worry, and her olive skin shimmered with sweat. She reached her arm up to wipe her forehead with the sleeve of her gray tunic, then guided her friend's hand down to touch the baby's head. *Why won't the baby come?* she wondered. She had been present during so many deliveries of women in her neighborhood, and she thought she had seen it all: every complication, every stage of labor.

She had been wrong.

This reality was a new one, and she was worried for her friend. The baby's head was visible, but it would not progress. *Why not?* she pondered, as a ripple of fear spread through her body. A new contraction began, and the midwife directed Anthia to support Dorema with both hands as she urged Dorema to push.

Anthia wanted to question the midwife directly: *How long has she been pushing? She started before dawn and now the sun is high in the sky. How long can a woman push? At what point does exhaustion take over, so that she can't continue?*

Dorema was a close friend. The two women had lived near each other for every one of their eighteen years, playing together as children, fetching water, helping to rear siblings, practicing their family trades, learning to cook, and then, later, becoming wives and mothers. This was Dorema's second childbirth experience. Her first baby was a girl, but Dorema's husband had not lifted the child from the ground, refusing to claim the girl as his child and raise her. At his direction the midwife had exposed the infant, leaving her in an area of Ephesus known for disposal of unwanted children. Anthia knew it was likely that a slaver had picked up the child, raising her until she was old enough to work and be sold.

ABORTION, INFANTICIDE, AND EXPOSURE

Abortion, infanticide, and exposure were practiced widely across the Roman Empire in the first century AD because of poverty, a preference for male children, poor contraception, doubtful parentage/legitimacy (including rape), physical deformity, an evil omen, and a desire for population control. These categories often overlapped; a family in poverty, for example, might expose or kill a female infant because the family's limited resources were understood to be better spent on a male infant.

Opinions varied among ancient philosophers and medical experts on when life began, though it was commonly argued that life began with delivery of the child (and its first breath, or even after it had lived up to forty days). Ancient Roman law did not classify a fetus as a person. Those who did oppose abortion often argued on the grounds of what was best for the state or empire rather than out of concern for the fetus, though Soranus of Ephesus (AD 98–137), a physician with an expertise in gynecology, stressed that abortion should only be allowed in cases where the mother's life was at risk.

Abortion was often attempted through the use of vaginal suppositories and potions (including the lupine plant and the plant species *Ecballium elaterium*, commonly called the squirting cucumber), though sometimes sharp objects were also used. Because of the dangers associated with abortion, however, infanticide (the killing of infants) and exposure were more common. The choice was almost always the father's, though the act itself would be carried out by a slave or midwife. Exposed infants were placed in baskets or pots and abandoned in a variety of places, ranging from deserted areas to public spaces known for exposure (especially in cities). These children died or were raised by slavers as commodities; occasionally they were adopted and raised as legitimate children.

These practices were legal in the ancient world because of the low societal value placed on children. Part of this value was a practical judgment, as only about half of children lived to their fifth birthday due mainly to malnutrition and disease. However, it is important to note that all Jewish and Christian literature available to us condemns these practices, and Roman writers who discuss the topic malign Jews for raising all the children that are born to them.

Dorema's cry brought Anthia's attention once again from the midwife to her friend. The midwife was placing a vulture feather under the birthing chair in hopes that it would ease the delivery. Anthia was hopeful at this activity, but then, other treatments had already been tried. It was several hours ago that Dorema had been drinking the urine of a female goat, and most recently it was a crushed insect rub that had been applied to her friend's body. Each of these treatments was supposed to help, but not one had. *Why not? What is the reason? Did we not give her enough urine to drink? Should we have mixed sow's milk with wine?* Then, suddenly, the answer hit her: *Artemis.* It was the goddess's choice that Dorema was suffering so terribly. It must be.

·   ■   ·

Anthia recalled the many trips to Artemis's temple that she and Dorema had made together, both for Dorema's first pregnancy and this one. Anthia's first baby was a boy. A *big* baby boy, whose entry had caused her own body much damage. She shuddered when she recalled the tearing and bleeding. It had been months before she was able to walk normally again. When she realized that she was pregnant again, her first reaction had been denial, as she remembered that she and Philetus had abstained from sex during the end of her period, the time when most doctors and midwives taught that women were fertile. They had even used honey as a contraceptive. After the denial came tears, and not tears of joy. The fear of having another labor and delivery like her first overwhelmed her initially. *Can my body survive an ordeal like that again? What if I tear again? How will I heal?* That fear also led her to petition Artemis even more fervently the second time around. Dorema had been a willing partner, as she had also recently realized that her second pregnancy was underway.

As their grandmothers and mothers had done before them, the two friends had petitioned Artemis and asked her to use her power on their behalf. *What had happened? Did we do something wrong? Did we not participate in enough ceremonies, sacrifices, processions, or celebrations of her birth?* She attempted to count the number of libations poured out—so much wine used, after all—but stopped short when she realized how small their efforts were when compared with the wealthy elite, who provided the music, dancers, sacrifices, feasts, and drinking parties in Artemis's honor. Her heart sank, then immediately lifted with hope. *Or perhaps I must petition her again, now, in this moment of childbirth?* Anthia and Dorema had prayed to Artemis together at the beginning of Dorema's labor, but perhaps it wasn't enough? Artemis needed more prayer? *I hope she doesn't require bread or coins or wine or incense; I have nothing to give.* She caught another glimpse of the metal mirror and was struck when she saw that the handle was an image of Artemis. *That's it*, she breathed silently. *Artemis is unhappy.*

Anthia's fear brought shivers down her spine. It was her fault. It must have been. She glanced around the room at the other women who were there to help with the labor and saw their worry, but she knew that her own anxiety far exceeded theirs. Another contraction gripped her friend, and Dorema's moan sounded different this time. Weaker. Alarmed, Anthia's eyes met the midwife's. They communicated wordlessly, then nodded. The baby needed to come out now.

ARTEMIS

In Greek mythology Artemis and her brother, Apollo, are born to Zeus and Leto. Artemis serves as her mother's midwife in this origin story, delivering her twin brother, Apollo. The Ephesians appropriated this myth and transferred its geographical location to a grove outside their city, a move that served to support their special relationship with Artemis. The Ephesian Artemis is thus a syncretized goddess, embodying features both of the classical Greek deity and a local goddess (or local goddesses). During the period of the New Testament, the historical evidence points to the likelihood of Ephesians hosting two major festivals in her honor every year. One was a celebration of her birth, complete with music, dancers, sacrifices, feasts, and priests acting out the role of demonic protectors of Artemis during her birth, frightening away the goddess Hera. The second was the Artemisia, which likely included competitions in music, theater, and athletics. There is also some evidence for female priestesses as officials of her temple.

Along with being associated with a general focus on health and safety (as her name was often understood to communicate those values), Artemis was acclaimed as greatest, holiest, and most manifest along with the

Anthia leaned in to whisper in her friend's ear: "Push, Dorema. Push. Harder!" Dorema's response was terrifying in its bleakness. She did not speak as the contraction seized her body; she did not respond at all. She did not push.

Anthia pushed on her friend's back, propping her up, while calling for two of the other women in the room to grab Dorema's hands on each side. "Tell her to push! Don't let her give up!"

titles "Queen of the Cosmos," "Lady" (female version of "Lord"), and "Savior." She was a specific kind of savior to the many women who petitioned her for safety in childbirth. She was the patron goddess of Ephesus, and her temple, the Artemision, was built outside the wall, a little over a mile from the city center. The Artemision was famous in antiquity, known as one of the seven wonders of the ancient world for its size and grandeur. It measured approximately 140 by 75 yards (four times the size of the Parthenon in Athens) and included 127 columns that stood over 60 feet high. The works of many of the greatest sculptors and painters of the day decorated it, and because of its financial deposits—assets that included land and water—and ability to lend money, it functioned at the center of the city's economic life.

Figure P.2. A statue of Artemis, the patron goddess of Ephesus

THE DANGERS OF LABOR,
CHILDBIRTH, AND INFANCY

Having a baby was the most dangerous experience that most women in the ancient world underwent. In the Roman Empire, as in most contexts throughout history, delivering babies was women's work. Midwives were almost always the primary medical caregiver during labor and delivery, and some had advanced medical training. They likely earned a decent living if they were free women rather than slaves.

Access to treatments for pain and ease in labor varied according to one's status and class, with poorer women often turning to superstition and folklore for support. Known treatments include herbs, animal dung, hyena's paw, snakeskin, or goose semen. These could be ingested or applied topically.

A typical life span for men across all social classes was about forty years, but for women it was closer to thirty years, and this was largely due to the dangers of childbearing. Most young women married after puberty, probably around age twelve to fourteen. Without reliable contraception, pregnancies were the result. Between 10 and 20 percent of mothers died in childbirth and its related complications.

Childbirth and its aftermath were also dangerous for the infant due to malnutrition, disease, and poor medical care. Mothers attempted to counteract this reality with a variety of spells, talismans, amulets, charms, and prayers, but only about two-thirds of children lived to age one, while only half of children survived their fifth birthday. An infant often was not counted as a live birth until it had survived for more than a week. The historical record gives examples of mothers whose survival rates for their children include one out of four or even one out of six. Because of this reality, some parents intentionally chose not to bond with young children, deferring affection and relationship until the children were older.

The women's encouraging words grew louder as they saw Dorema's lack of response. Soon Anthia found that she was yelling into her friend's ear. "Push! Push! You're so close! Push!" She could hear the terror in her voice, and as it overtook her a small part of her knew that she was watching her friend die. "No! Breathe!" she screamed, grabbing Dorema's shoulders and shaking them. Dorema's body was limp, not responding to Anthia or the other women. She said nothing.

Anthia moved to face her friend, and when she saw Dorema's face she had the distinct sense that her friend was giving up. The look reminded her of her own labor and delivery. With her first child, her belly had been huge, and her labor long and intense. When she was finally instructed by the midwife to push, she could barely muster the energy. After a few hours of pushing, she was done. She could not push anymore. She recalled her awareness in that moment, as she had not pushed during the entire course of a contraction: *I am dying. I am not pushing— cannot push—and I am allowing myself to die.*

It had been Dorema in that moment who had rallied her, called her back, insisted that she push one more time. The baby had come.

As if in response to her thoughts, the unborn child in her own womb kicked, and Anthia touched her own protruding belly with one hand. She grabbed her friend's chin with the other. "Dorema, look at me! Look at me!" Dorema's only response was to gaze past her and exhale. Anthia waited for the inhale, holding her friend's face.

It never came.

Day 1, Wednesday

DAY OF MERCURY/HERMES

A FEW DAYS LATER, ANTHIA WALKED SLOWLY with her husband, Philetus, and son, Nikias, in the agora. They were on their way home and had just left their small vendor space, the place where Anthia and some of the other wives sold the fish their husbands caught. It had been a slow morning, and she was sure that the poor business was compounded by the recent spate of accusations in Ephesus against fishmongers. Some had been accused of selling inferior and even rotten fish at high prices, and that perception had spread to the larger populace; Anthia and the other women were working hard to dispel the notion by providing high-quality fish.

The men had caught so few fish in their nets, just some small anchovies and sardines. They had tried for the bigger fish in the harbor, including tuna, but had not been successful. Their fishing was not going well in general lately, and Anthia knew that Philetus and his *koinonoi*, partners, were worried.

Anthia had her own ideas about where the fish had gone, but she did not dare say anything. Of course, the bigger question remained, *Where might we find food?* Anthia's stomach rumbled, and when she touched her belly, the baby kicked. *Yes, you are hungry as well*, she thought.

It was late morning, time for rest and food, the latter for those who could afford it. Her family usually ate two meals per day, if they were lucky. Last year, her husband had hoped to improve their situation and status by joining with other local fishermen in an association. The association had given them the ability to bid for fishing contracts from wealthy families as well as contracts with salting houses. The association also helped its members manage the relentless taxation of the Romans. The Romans controlled the harbor, and those who fished in it owed steep taxes on everything they caught. In a public declaration of the importance of the fishing profession in Ephesus and their ability to pay their taxes, their association had contributed toward the building and dedication of the new fishery toll office. They also had, quite appropriately, set up a monument listing the names and status of the contributors.

Anthia smiled when she pictured her husband's name near the bottom, after the Roman citizens. *Philetus. Free man. 6 denaria.* She knew that the association was unusual in its membership, as most guilds were composed of people from the same class and status level. Theirs was intentionally mixed, and she was grateful to the Roman citizens who had been willing to form an association that welcomed fishermen and fishmongers from further down the status ladder.

It had been a time of such pride and honor. But now things were different. *How will we survive?* she wondered. *The catch is so small most days, and after selling the fish and paying the taxes, there is not much left.* They usually kept a couple of small fish for their family, to guarantee that they would have something to eat that day. But the income from selling the rest paid their rent and gave them the ability to buy cloth, fuel for cooking, and other food. Mostly they lived on grains, olive oil, vinegar, diluted wine, and lentils or beans. A real treat was a fresh vegetable or piece of fruit.

ASSOCIATIONS

In the ancient Greco-Roman world, the various levels of government often operated in a symbiotic relationship with local voluntary associations. In other words, the associations offered many people an entry point into a community of people who could pool their resources (financial, social, and otherwise) toward the greater goals of a guild, religion, social club, or city. From the evidence we have, it appears that most members of voluntary associations were male, though there are exceptions. It is likely that the earliest local "churches" would have been understood within this framework (as well as the framework of the Jewish synagogue) both by insiders—members as followers of Jesus—and outsiders.

Figure 1.1. The monument erected by the fishers' and fishmongers' association in the 50s CE

There was an actual guild association of fishers and fishmongers at Ephesus in the 50s AD that was composed of people (along with their families) who represented a fairly wide spectrum of socioeconomic levels. They built a monument that celebrated their membership in the association as well as their work in building the fishery toll office. The monument lists approximately one hundred names that include Roman citizens (at least forty-three), persons free or freed from slavery (between thirty-six and forty-one), and slaves (between two and ten). The donors are listed according to the size of their contribution, with top donors first. The amounts range from the amount required to provide four marble columns to a sum of less than five denaria, or five days' wages for a day laborer.

The noises of vendors hawking their goods mixed with the laughter of children and the sounds of sheep, pigs, and wild dogs. Anthia let her mind wander as she walked, and as they passed Dorema's favorite vegetable stall she was hit once again with the realization that Dorema was dead. A wave of grief covered her, drowning out the noise of the busy marketplace.

Her haze of grief was halted by the cry of Nikias. She stopped walking, her eyes searching for her son. *There he is.* His dark hair flopped over his equally dark eyes, and his small, naked body was crunched into a ball on the ground. She walked several steps back, to where he was sitting and clutching his bleeding knee. Bending over was awkward with her belly protruding, but she did so quickly, scooping him up while making soothing sounds. He insisted that she kiss his knee, and she did, wiping the blood from his olive skin with her hand and offering up a quick prayer of thanks to the gods for his health and vitality. *Almost three years old, and so strong. His name was well chosen; he is truly victorious.* Though Nikias insisted on being carried through the busy area, she set him down next to her and grabbed his little hand instead. "Your brother in my belly is taking up all of mommy's space," she told him. "Soon I will hold both of you, one in each arm. Soon, my little victory."

They passed a shop displaying burial items, and her grief returned. She noticed the same type of tombstone that marked Dorema and her tiny daughter's grave outside the city. After Dorema's death, the midwife had followed accepted practice and cut the baby out of the womb. But it had been too late. The child was stillborn.

Dorema's family had scraped together enough money to purchase the gravestone and pay for the engraving, though they had not been able to pay what it cost to commemorate Dorema or the baby properly. Anthia had done what she could; she had assisted

Dorema's mother and sister in washing, oiling, and wrapping the bodies. She had stood with family and friends at the wake, as Dorema's body lay, her infant daughter next to her, with her feet pointed toward the door in the one-room home Dorema had shared with her husband, his brother, and his brother's family. In contrast to the tears of the women, however, Dorema's husband had stood stoically. Anthia knew that he was a man of few words and that he had not been affectionate toward his wife. Dorema also had not felt affection for her husband. She had simply accepted her father's wishes and married the man of his choosing.

She shook her head to clear it and tried reminding herself of what everyone knew—that pregnancy and childbirth were dangerous, and everyone had friends and family who had not survived them—but it didn't help. She was careful to keep her emotions veiled, however, and maintain her composure. A public display of grief would shame and anger her husband.

He was a good man, taking seriously his responsibility to care for her. Anthia was his second wife, his first having died in childbirth. She had heard that his first marriage was largely a product of his father's wishes, though she did not doubt that he had cared for his first wife in ways that were similar to how he treated her. Their own marriage had been initiated by him; she had noticed his eyes on her during festival meals and in the agora, or marketplace, and she was pleasantly surprised when he had approached her father. They were social peers, sharing the same status, and the match had pleased families on both sides. At the time she had been fourteen years old, and he twenty-eight. She was ready for marriage and the responsibility of caring for a home, as her mother had trained her well. While Philetus occasionally hit or pushed her, she knew that it could be much worse, and she was grateful to be married to a man who did indeed care about and for her by providing for her needs. Their household felt secure to Anthia. They were doing their part for the honor of Ephesus, the province of Asia, and the Roman empire.

As they exited the agora, Anthia noticed a crowd gathered outside a nearby building. It caught her husband's attention as

MARRIAGE

In the Roman Empire a healthy household was considered to be the foundation for a healthy society. Marriage for nonelites (who comprised most of the population in the Roman Empire) was a family matter, not a governmental concern. This was due largely to the lack of money for a dowry or legal inheritance. In such situations the man and woman simply agreed that they wished to be married to each other, each stating "yes," and their community accepted it. There were no prewritten vows or religious aspects. They would celebrate with friends and family and set up a home together.

A good wife was expected to be loyal in everything. Loyalty to one's husband included being chaste until marriage, following his gods, obeying him, demonstrating modesty, not courting attention from other men, showing affection in bed to him as her only sexual partner, and allowing him to have other sexual partners without penalty. It was only adultery if a husband's sexual partners included other men's wives. The wife's loyalty extended to her husband's parents and family as well. There was a great deal of social pressure on wives to live up to these expectations, and most wives fell in line.

Social expectations for husbands included providing clothing and other necessities for their wives, teaching wives the family trade, and being discreet in their sexual liaisons. Physical and sexual abuse by husbands was common and socially accepted.

well, and he signaled his intention to take a closer look. Public speakers and philosophers were common in Ephesus at lecture halls like this one, but this was an odd time of day for teaching students. Most teachers were busy in the early mornings, not during the midday break.

The group standing outside was silent, listening intently to the discussion inside. Anthia and Philetus joined them, and Anthia found herself standing on tiptoe to see better. The voices of two men emerged, and one had an accent that identified him as a foreigner. Where had she heard that accent before? *The linen trader from Rome? The gladiator from Macedonia?* she pondered.

The foreigner was talking about having hope after death. *Hope after death?* thought Anthia. *What hope is there? My friend is lost forever to Hades. I will never see her again.* Still, her curiosity about this hope overrode her better judgment, and she continued to listen.

The man's dialogue partner apparently had the same thought, because he then asked the foreigner how there could possibly be any hope after death. The accented voice replied that resurrection was possible. He clarified that resurrection did not mean that one's soul or spirit lived on but that a person would be brought back to life in a restored body. *Body?!* considered Anthia. *Ridiculous. Everyone knows that dead people don't come back to life, much less in their bodies.* Again, the Ephesian man's reaction mirrored Anthia's, and he stated his skepticism of such an idea, asking how it could be possible.

The other man then told the story of a man named Jesus who had died and been brought back to life—resurrected—in a restored body. "Even if that happened, which I doubt, that does not explain how or why it gives hope after death for the rest of us," the local man argued. "Paul," he continued, "what kind of philosophy is this? I know of none that include this idea. All the philosophical systems I am familiar with do not value the physical body at all but prioritize the spirit and hope for it to be free from the body."

Anthia nodded her head in agreement. Even she knew that much. The body was lesser, dirty, even evil. The spirit was what mattered. She inched her way forward, inserting herself between two other women who were watching, and saw the man Paul and his debate partner for the first time. Paul was not what she expected. *Average, normal*, she thought. He was probably five foot three, thin yet muscular, with a beard, and dark hair and eyes. *Looks like most people around here. Actually, he looks quite similar to Philetus. Same broad nose and thick eyebrows. It's just his accent that gives him away.*

Paul's next response only added to Anthia's surprise and confusion. "The true god of the world," declared Paul, "is the one who created all things, including humans. That god sent Jesus as the new man to show all of us how to truly live, and those who commit to Jesus and honor him with their lives will be raised into resurrected bodies as he was."

"Who is this man Paul?" Anthia's husband asked an acquaintance also standing outside the lecture hall.

"He is part of a movement called 'the Way,' a sect of the Jewish faith. He was teaching and dialoguing in the Jewish synagogue until his own kind kicked him out. He moved here, to Tyrannus's lecture hall, and has continued promoting his crazy ideas."

A Jew? That helped to explain the strangeness of what Anthia had just heard. She knew little of Jews, but she was aware that they oddly worshiped only one god. The Jews could not even see their god, as they had no statues or images of him. They also had unusual food laws, circumcised their baby boys, and had a lazy day once every seven days. But this, this resurrection idea was a new one. She'd have to talk with her neighbors about it later. Her friend Eutaxia would definitely know more details; she was always up to date on the news in the area.

Philetus nodded to her, and Anthia adjusted her grip on Nikias's hand and followed. It was time to rest.

■ ■ ■

In the small room they called home, Anthia sat on the floor near the others who shared the space, including her father, aunt, and sister-in-law. Anthia pulled apart a small piece of dark, flat bread. She placed some in Nikias's eager hand, then offered the rest to Philetus, who took it and tore it yet again. He shook his head, mentioned her belly, and handed a small section of the bread back to her. Anthia knew that the baby inside her needed some nourishment, so she ate the few bites. She dipped them in garum, a fish sauce. As she ate, she offered up a silent prayer to Poseidon's wife, Amphitrite, the goddess queen of the sea. *O Amphitrite, you who spawn all the fish of the sea, send a school to my husband's nets.*

Amphitrite could perhaps be persuaded by an offering or libation, though Anthia knew that the food or wine needed for such rites would be expensive. She and her family were hungry, but of course it could be much worse. They were surrounded by others in similar situations: friends, neighbors, and strangers who were focused on survival. A famine, a political crisis, a surge of new residents to their already packed *insula*, or apartment building—any of these realities, and others, could make it harder for them to sustain their lives.

Her eyes met those of her sister-in-law. Even after all this time Penelope's blue eyes still caught Anthia's attention. Penelope's grandfather had been brought to Ephesus as a slave from a barbarian land, and her eyes and light hair were inherited from him. Penelope was also chewing slowly, savoring a few bites of the other piece of bread. Her two children ate hungrily, one at her breast and one sitting on the floor. The shared glance communicated volumes. Both women knew there was nothing they could do in that moment to provide more food for their children. Anthia glanced next at her father and aunt, who were both sitting in their favorite corners on bedmats. Neither was eating, and the reason was clear. There was not enough food to go around. At least Penelope's husband, Andrew, wasn't here, as he would simply be another mouth to feed. Andrew worked as a day laborer in the harbor and rarely returned home midday.

Finally, Anthia cleared her throat. "How was your morning, Penelope?" She was almost afraid to ask but felt she needed to do so. The quick shake of Penelope's head told her everything she needed to know. It was the season of harvest, and these days Penelope spent her mornings outside the city, attempting to glean whatever wheat, barley, beans, or lentils she could from already-harvested fields. Her task was complicated by her need to nurse her infant, who cried constantly and was quieted only when nursing. She usually wore him, wrapped near her breast, to keep her hands free. The toddler had been staying behind with Anthia's father and aunt, but her father was old and frail. It was often her aunt, Eirene, who cared both for Anthia's father, Demas, and the toddler while Penelope was in the fields.

While Anthia reached for a plain ceramic cup, she considered the bowl that sat next to it, which during times of plenty was often full of barley soaking in water. The soaked barley would then be used to make porridge or the chewy dark bread they often ate. At least they had enough water to drink; there were lead-pipe open aqueducts in the city, some of which brought water from rivers that were miles away. There was also a spring, the Callipia, inside the city, and fountains throughout, one of which was nearby. Anthia knew that the elite terraced apartments

POVERTY AND SUBSISTENCE

New Testament scholar Steven Friesen has famously proposed a seven-tiered "poverty scale" for the free (i.e., not slave) population of the Roman Empire.[a] Others have modified and nuanced his work (including Bruce Longenecker), but the basic paradigm is still helpful.[b] Perhaps the top 3 percent of the Roman empire was part of the social elite and lived well above any ancient poverty line, with access to a great deal of excess of whatever resources (including food) they desired.

The rest—97 percent—of the free population was spread across a wide range in terms of access to food and other necessities. The top percentage of this large majority would have had access to some surplus that would have helped them to survive famines and other shortages. Perhaps traders, veterans, some farmers, merchants, and artisans would fit this category, and their numbers are estimated anywhere from 7 to 17 percent.

The bottom 80 to 90 percent of the population lived just above, at, or below the subsistence level, with subsistence defined as the minimum needed to sustain life. Farm families as well as some traders, shop owners, laborers, small-scale merchants, and artisans would have lived at the top and middle of this group, with prisoners, the disabled, unskilled day laborers, beggars, and unattached orphans and widows at the bottom end.

---

[a]Steven J. Friesen, "Poverty in Pauline Studies: Beyond the So-Called New Consensus," *Journal for the Study of the New Testament* 26, no. 3 (2004): 323-61.
[b]Bruce Longenecker, *Remember the Poor* (Grand Rapids: Eerdmans, 2010).

near the lower agora each had water funneled to them through an elaborate and costly system. Their own *insula* did not have such a structure, but she was content to carry water from the fountain up the stairs every day.

She heard a child cry. *Euxinus*, she thought, and smiled, recognizing the sound of her friend Eutaxia's son next door. They lived on the top floor of a multistory *insula*, and the walls were thin. Their area of Ephesus was filled with *insulae*, which housed laborers of all kinds, artisans, small-shop and tavern owners, and various merchants and traders. Some higher-status people also lived in *insulae*, though they often lived in several rooms, not just one, like Anthia and her family. *It's not that crowded*, she told herself. *There are only nine of us in this room. Well . . . ten, counting you.* She patted her belly.

She laid Nikias down on the small mat in one corner, taking her place next to him. Philetus quickly joined them, and Penelope copied the action, lying down nearby with her boys. Anthia looked toward her father and aunt, but they were already resting. She listened to the noise of the neighboring apartments; Eutaxia and her husband were arguing again, and the new baby in the room below them was crying. A goat bleated from somewhere, and a child was singing. She dozed, only to be awakened by the sharp kick of the baby inside her. She touched her stomach. *Baby, all is well. Rest.* The kicks continued at a furious rate. Smiling, she added, *You must be a boy. A strong, healthy boy. Artemis, great goddess, please smile upon me and shape the form of this child in my womb to be male. Please.* Knowing that she had work to do, she struggled to sit up, though the size of her belly impeded quick movement.

As she stood, her foot accidentally kicked the ceramic cup she had used earlier, and it broke into several pieces that scattered on the floor. She sank to her knees and began to scoop up the shards with her fingers, but Philetus's backhand on her cheek stopped her. Half kneeling, she paused before giving the expected response.

"So sorry. This is my fault, and I will fix it." She waited, not daring to touch her stinging cheek in front of him.

"Clean it up and come." She did so, making sure to pick up each fragment. Grabbing Nikias from his mat, she managed to snatch her cloak as well before she moved toward the door with her husband.

They walked down the flights of stairs that led from their *insula* to the street, with Anthia doing her best to hide her red face from those they met on the way. Once outside, she adjusted her cloak to cover her head and face.

She walked quickly, matching her pace to that of her husband. The smell of sewage intensified as they neared the public latrines, though the streets always smelled of both human and animal excrement and urine. They passed a man relieving himself on a wall, and he stumbled backward, narrowly missing them with his stream of urine.

Near the agora they again walked past the lecture hall of Tyrannus. The crowd outside was still there, and even from a distance Anthia could hear the agitated voices.

"Paul, you insult me! Surely no educated man in Asia could believe such nonsense! You say that the one true god of the world has appointed this man Jesus as judge over all of us and that his resurrection is proof of this?"

Paul's response was equally passionate. "Yes! And the appropriate response is repentance, which means giving up our own agendas and priorities and living as this god created us to live!"

Anthia and her husband passed behind the crowd silently, listening to the heated debate. Philosophical debate was nothing new in Ephesus; to the contrary, it was a valued activity and showcased the education and status of its participants. What was new was the content. Resurrection? Repentance? Judgment? Though he was clearly educated, perhaps the mind of that man Paul was not healthy. *That must be it*, Anthia assured herself. *He's unwell.* She found that she was still listening, however, even as the voices faded. *Well, that's that*, she concluded. *No more of Paul.*

Back in their fishmonger's stall, Philetus conferred with a few other men and left with them to fish. Anthia watched them go, wondering where they would fish and which gods they might petition on the way. She settled in with the other women, glancing up at their few small fish that had been hung to display them to anyone interested in buying or trading.

■   ■   ■

A few hours later, Philetus had returned, and Anthia followed him out of their fish stall and into the market, grabbing Nikias's hand on the way. The women had successfully traded the fish for some olives and chickpeas. *At least we'll have something to eat tonight*, she thought, *even though the men did not catch any new fish this afternoon.*

And then a familiar voice caught her attention: "Yes, of course! Priscilla, Aquila, we can manage that, don't you think?"

Startled, Anthia turned her head to see the man Paul from the lecture hall. He was standing in a small shop with another man and woman, and they were holding what appeared to be leather of some kind. She heard his accent again as he continued talking with a third man, who was clearly a potential customer. "Hippothous, we will make this tent for you. And won't you eat with us this evening as well?" Hippothous's reply was too quiet to hear, but Paul's response was not. His laughter filled the air, and he clapped his customer on the back. "That is true, but it does not matter. We can still eat together, and Aquila and Priscilla will be there as well. Jesus, whom we worship and honor, shared meals with people from varying status levels, and we do the same."

Shocked, Anthia continued to walk next to her husband. She glanced at his face, but he apparently hadn't overheard the conversation. *Eating with people who outrank you? Or whom you outrank? What can he be thinking?* wondered Anthia. *Who does such a thing? And why?* She pondered the question of whether Paul was trying to gain honor by eating with someone from a higher status than him. *Could that be it?* Then Paul's answer came back to her: *Jesus. Paul had said that he eats like Jesus ate.* Jesus was also the one Paul had said was raised from the dead, so Anthia knew that she couldn't trust what Paul said. But maybe tomorrow she would listen carefully as she passed the lecture hall and the shop; perhaps she could discover more. At the very least, it was good gossip.

Day 2, Thursday

Day of Jupiter/Zeus

Just before dawn Anthia rose from her bedmat. She couldn't lie there anymore, let alone sleep. *My hips hurt so much,* she mourned silently. *I haven't had this many aches since the last time I was pregnant.* She knew that the pain in her hips was part of her body's process to prepare for the delivery, but the knowledge did little to console her. Her most comfortable position these past weeks was standing, as lying down on her side hurt her hips, while lying on her back made it difficult to breathe. Sitting on the floor squished her belly, also making it difficult to breathe. Even standing, however, had its limits, because after a few minutes her lower back started to hurt. She quietly poured some water into a small ceramic cup and sipped.

Nikias stirred under his blanket, and Anthia resisted the urge to lean over and touch him. *If I bend down over him, I might never get back up. Besides, he needs his sleep,* she told herself. Their meals may be unpredictable and often too small, but at least she could give him the sleep he needed. So many children did not live beyond these early years, and Anthia was determined to do everything in her power to help her son survive even if disease and hunger stalked them.

Wet. Her mind registered the feeling, but it took a moment for Anthia to understand fully what was happening. *I'm dripping.* Her arms felt like wooden planks as she reached for the bottom half of her tunic and pulled it up. She attempted to bend so that she could see her thighs, but the size of her belly made it impossible. Frustrated, she touched her leg. *Wet.* Pulling her fingers back, she inspected them in the predawn light. Blood covered them. Then, as if on cue, a dull pain blossomed in her pelvis, spreading throughout her lower abdomen.

She glanced at Philetus and was relieved to see him sleeping on his side with his back toward her. Her father, aunt, and brother-in-law's family were also still. Discreetly, she grabbed the clay chamber pot and crouched over it, considering her situation. She hadn't ever bled during pregnancy, so this was not a good sign. It was too early for the baby to come, so the bleeding could not indicate a healthy labor. *Am I losing the baby?* Fear gripped her, and she prayed a silent prayer to Artemis for protection. Philetus stirred, and she quickly leaned over to her stock of rags, folding one into a rectangle and placing it carefully into her *subligacula*, the cloth she wore wrapped between her legs and around her hips. *I'm low on rags*, she realized, making a mental note to ask Eutaxia for more.

■ ■ ■

Everyone was drinking water. Anthia glanced at her husband, and he smiled when his eyes met hers. *Should I tell him? Or any of them? Maybe Penelope . . .* She wasn't sure what to do. It probably didn't help that she couldn't breathe very well while sitting on the floor like this, but she was afraid that if she stood the blood might run down her legs to the floor. At least this way she could keep a rag in place.

Nikias looked at her hungrily, then his eyes moved from her face to the bowl that often held the barley porridge. It was empty. *What will we do?* She wished that she could nurse him, but he had been weaned for almost a year. Perhaps she should have hired out her services as a wet nurse when her breasts were still producing milk. Then she likely wouldn't have gotten pregnant again either. She sighed. *Too late. There is nothing to be done.* Philetus hadn't been thrilled at the idea of her being a wet nurse, as it was such an obvious indicator of poverty and low status. And at the time, the fish had been plentiful. She and the other women had been so busy in the agora selling the catch their husbands caught each day that Anthia hadn't had the time to be a wet nurse. She caught herself watching her sister-in-law as she nursed the baby, and for a fleeting moment she pondered asking Penelope to nurse Nikias for a moment.

No, she decided. *I can't. Penelope hasn't eaten either. It would be cruel to ask her body to nurse another child.*

Philetus cleared his throat. "Galleos and I caught nothing last night. We are going to try another new spot in the harbor this morning." Anthia nodded, her face a mask of calm. She dared not reveal even a hint of her true thoughts regarding Galleos. *Weasel.* She had always thought that he had been named after an appropriate animal. He was small in stature, and Anthia's friends agreed that his very demeanor was predatory. His eyes always followed the women, tracing their bodies. Anthia had also over-heard him making vulgar jokes.

With that short statement, Philetus stood, adjusted his belt, and left. Andrew was already gone; he had left while it was still dark, hoping to be at the front of the line for day laborers looking for work. Her father moved to lie back down on his mat, and Anthia knew her aunt would stay to attend him. Penelope stood, pulled her child from her breast, and handed him wordlessly to

Anthia. Both women understood the reality; Penelope needed to go outside the city once again to attempt to find food in the fields, and Anthia would stay with the children. She needed to be near in case the men caught fish. However, with no fish to sell this morning, Anthia would be able to visit Eutaxia. As she stood, she again felt the blood run down her leg. *I will talk to Eutaxia about this*, she decided. Eutaxia's mother had been a respected midwife, and she had been training her daughter when she had suddenly fallen ill and died last year. *Eutaxia will know what to do.*

· · ·

Anthia adjusted her shoulders and looked at Phoebe and Eutaxia, her two closest friends. "When did the bleeding start?" Phoebe asked.

"Please, Phoebe," Anthia whispered, even as she admired again her friend's thick, curly brown hair. The knot at the back of her head could not contain it, and it sprouted curly wings that framed Phoebe's face. All three women actually looked remarkably similar. *We could be sisters*, Anthia had often thought. *We all have dark hair, eyes, skin, and light builds. But the hair... Phoebe's hair is so beautiful.* Phoebe blushed and looked furtively to her left, to the thin wall shared with Eutaxia's nosy neighbor. The elderly woman next door lived with her adult son and his family, and she was often home during the day with the youngest two children while everyone else was working.

Anthia was grateful to be with friends. The three of them had grown up together in Ephesus in the same *insula*, and Eutaxia and Anthia were still neighbors, living in side-by-side one-room apartments on the top floor of an *insula*, largely because their husbands were cousins and had wanted to live near each other. Phoebe, however, now lived a few streets over. Phoebe was a few years older and had given birth to three children, two of whom survived. Her first, a boy, had died after three days, six days before his naming day. Her second child was a girl, and Phoebe's husband had lifted her from the ground and chosen to raise her. The third, another boy, was swaddled in Phoebe's arms.

"This morning. I got up early because my hips hurt, and as I stood I felt the bleeding start." Anthia paused anxiously, raising her eyebrows in question as she looked back and forth at the faces of her two friends.

URBAN HOUSING

Though only a small percentage of the population in the Roman Empire in the first century lived in cities (perhaps 10 to 15 percent), the housing was often compact. *Insulae*, or a type of ancient apartment building, housed most of the population, with the same building often inhabited by people from a cross section of the status and class spectrum. *Insulae* often stood four to five stories tall, and the cheapest and most dangerous apartments were those on the top floor, where the structural defects of thin walls and poor building materials placed occupants at the greatest risk from collapse or fire.

While the wealthy may have lived in apartments with multiple rooms, most people lived as extended families in just one room that may have averaged about one hundred square feet. Because there were few windows, the rooms were often dark and damp, and the poor ventilation and lack of running water spread disease. While there were some well-constructed *insulae* in Ephesus that used a pipe system for running water (and housed only the wealthy), most apartment dwellers used public fountains and carried water up the stairs in buckets. The presence of cesspits for human waste at the bottom floor also contributed

Eutaxia's response was direct and clinical. "How much blood? How many rags have you used?" Anthia wished that she would be a little more compassionate, but compassion was not Eutaxia's strength.

"I'm still on my first."

Eutaxia's curt nod accompanied her analysis. "It's not good, but it could be worse. Your belly is big, and the baby is growing, but he isn't ready to be born. He won't survive if he comes now.

to disease, as did the waste in the streets. Chamber pots were supposed to be emptied into the cesspits (which were often bins), but contents were often tossed out of windows at night.

Of course, some city dwellers did not have access to housing, and they sheltered in storerooms under stairs or bridges, tombs, basements, public lavatories or baths, or temple porches.

Figure 2.1. The remains of an ancient *insula*, a type of apartment building

We have to try to stop the bleeding. Can you feel him moving and kicking?"

At this new question, Anthia paused to consider. She hadn't even thought about her baby's movement because the bleeding had worried her so much. "I haven't felt him move today, or at least I don't remember him moving," she admitted.

Her friend's worried look told her all she needed to know. At Eutaxia's direction, Anthia stretched out on the small mat on the floor and tried to get comfortable. Lying on her back was not an option; she could hardly breathe with the weight of her belly constricting her lungs. She moved to her side and rested her head on her arm, barely moving it in time to miss a small foot that was running by.

The four toddlers were playing some kind of chasing game, and that ruckus, combined with the fussing of Phoebe's baby, made Anthia wish they could go outside. At least Penelope's baby was sleeping, bundled tightly in rags in the corner. And they had a lot of natural light, because while there was only one small window, there were multiple holes in the outside wall. Eutaxia covered them at night with scraps of fabric, but during the day the added light was a bonus.

Eutaxia walked to one wall and poured a small amount of wine from an amphora into a ceramic cup. She handed it to Anthia, then sat down. Anthia sipped the wine gratefully and watched Eutaxia mend her son's small tunic. "Isn't that the tunic you just made?" asked Phoebe.

"Yes, from Lampo's old one. He laughed when Lykos tore it yesterday, saying that our son is indeed a wolf." She shook her head. "I may need to go to the agora for some thread. Perhaps I can trade a few olives for it."

"Speaking of the agora, have you heard of the man Paul, who teaches and dialogues in the lecture hall of Tyrannus near the gate of Mazeus and Mithridates?" Anthia asked. Both women nodded, with Eutaxia exclaiming in consternation.

"I heard about him from a miller, who has some Jewish customers who buy her flour. They told her that he came to Ephesus several months ago and focused on the Jews only. He spent a lot of time in their homes and synagogue, discussing something called 'the Way' with them."

Figure 2.2. The gate of Mazeus and Mithridates (right) was built in AD 40 by two slaves, Mazeus and Mithridates, who had been freed. The gate is dedicated to the emperor Caesar Augustus and his family. The structure on the left is the Celsus Library and was built in the early second century AD, after Paul's visits to Ephesus.

"What is that?" Phoebe adjusted her breast as she lifted her *strophium*, her breast cloth, and angled her nipple toward her infant son's crying mouth. "I have never heard of it, and when I listened to Paul debate another philosopher a few days ago outside the hall, he did not mention it."

"One of the Jewish holy texts mentions the *way* of their god," Eutaxia proudly announced. Shocked, Phoebe and Anthia stared at their friend. "In this scroll one of their prophets tells of a time when their god will comfort them and restore their good fortune after disciplining them. When the god comes to do this, his *way* is to be prepared by his people, those who honor him," Eutaxia added. "And the man Paul claims that this god is doing it now, which means that there are already those who are part of his way. Others can join if they wish." Eutaxia exhaled and smiled smugly.

"Have you been debating with Paul in the lecture hall?" asked Phoebe sarcastically. "You are truly an expert."

"I just keep my ears open," Eutaxia retorted. "I was at the baths yesterday and ended up next to a slave of a wealthy Jewish woman. The slave's mistress is a student of Paul's and is convinced that what he says is true. She has helped to pay for his use of the lecture hall so that others can learn from him."

"I heard him yesterday," Anthia admitted. "Philetus and I stopped to listen to him after our morning work. He was talking about the strangest thing, something called resurrection. It means being raised to life after death. It's not just your spirit but your body."

"How can that be?" Phoebe mused. "And why would anyone want to be in a body? I cannot wait to escape this shell. Having babies has not improved it; I am so soft and saggy in many places, and I need to visit the latrine more often than before." Eutaxia and Anthia laughed knowingly.

"Anthia still wins," Eutaxia claimed. "Her injuries after Nikias were so great that she could not walk normally for months." Anthia merely nodded in assent, not wanting to discuss it. She worked hard to keep the vivid flashbacks from coming, as they caused her heart to race and her body to break into a sweat.

"It could have been worse," Anthia asserted. To herself she added, *I could have died.* She took a deep breath and continued. "That's why Paul's words caught my attention. He said there is hope, and that death does not win, does not have to win. He mentioned another Jewish man named Jesus who was the first to be raised from the dead. Paul said that Jesus conquered death! Could it be?"

"Impossible," Phoebe argued. "If something like that were true, wouldn't our great philosophers have known it long ago? These new ideas can't be trusted."

"I agree, but it's still interesting." Eutaxia's eyes danced mischievously. "And when prominent people like that wealthy Jewish woman join, it makes for good gossip. I'm going to get thread for mending; do you two mind staying with Euxinus for a bit?" They nodded their agreement, and as Eutaxia walked through the doorway she added, "And I'll be sure to walk by Tyrannus's lecture hall on the way."

■　■　■

While they waited for Eutaxia to return, Anthia and Phoebe talked quietly, and the children ate. Anthia resisted the urge to cry as she watched Nikias gulp down his simple meal of millet flat cake and olive oil. "Thank you," she said again.

Phoebe's only response was to insist that she eat a few bites. "You need to eat as well. The baby needs nourishment, and perhaps some good food and rest will help the bleeding to stop." Gratefully, Anthia accepted a piece of the flat cake and dipped it in oil. She longed for a turnip, onion, or a few bites of chickpeas, but it was not to be. She sent up a silent prayer of thanks for Phoebe and her generosity. They were not only friends but distant relatives as well, and their shared kinship meant that they often shared resources. It was about survival, and everyone took care of their own. Anthia glanced through a crack in the wall toward the sun; it was much higher in the sky, which meant that Eutaxia had been gone for quite a while. "Where could she be?" Anthia asked.

Just then Eutaxia burst through the wooden door triumphantly, her right hand extended. In it was a treat that instantly made Anthia's mouth water. "Sausage! Where did you get that?"

"From the slave that I mentioned earlier, Rhoda. Her mistress, the wealthy Jewish woman, bought several for herself and Rhoda. I saw them standing outside of the lecture hall listening to Paul. Rhoda shared one with me."

Eutaxia broke the sausage into bites and gave each woman and child one. The taste of pork offal and spices exploded in Anthia's mouth, and she nodded appreciatively at Eutaxia. Eutaxia's smile answered her as she picked up her son and began to nurse him. Eutaxia's son Euxinus was her third child; the first two had not lived to their naming days. Euxinus was now two years old and would be weaned soon, though Anthia knew that his weak health concerned his mother, who petitioned the gods regularly for strength and life on behalf of her son.

"Well, how was the agora?" Phoebe's question hung in the air, and Eutaxia pasted on an innocent expression.

"What do you mean?"

"Don't play that game with us," Phoebe warned, though her laughter demonstrated her true feelings. "Tell us."

"So today Paul was talking about all the different peoples and nations. He was answering questions from the men who were listening, but then Rhoda's mistress asked one! In front of everyone, she asked about what the man Jesus means for the way that Jews interact with other people groups and nations." Anthia involuntarily held her breath, marveling at the status and power some women possessed.

"And?" Phoebe prompted, when Eutaxia paused a bit too long.

"Well, first, he called her by name—Dorcas—so he knows her. And then he said that Jesus was god's way of bringing all the peoples, nations, tribes, and clans together. Jesus is the first new human, and a new humanity and unity for all people is possible through him." Eutaxia shook her head wonderingly. "The craziest part wasn't even what he was saying, it was the way he said it. He was so excited, so joyful. I don't understand."

"How?" Anthia questioned. "How does Jesus create a new humanity and unity among people?"

"Paul talked a lot about the peace and reconciliation that Jesus brings, peace that overcomes hostility between different peoples."

Peace, thought Anthia. Now that was a word she had heard often from the Roman citizens who lived in Ephesus. The Roman Empire had brought peace to all, they claimed. "So the peace that Jesus brings, is it like the Roman peace? Does he reconcile people to each other like the Romans do, by conquering all and enforcing Roman law?"

"No," Eutaxia countered, "Paul made a big point of saying that Jesus' peace is not forced. It's peace between people and reconciliation to the god who sent Jesus, and . . ." Eutaxia paused for dramatic effect.

"And what?" Phoebe demanded. Anthia smiled at the way that Eutaxia consistently aggravated Phoebe, though Phoebe always pushed back in her own way.

"And . . . Jesus made this possible by dying on a cross."

The women were silent as Phoebe and Anthia digested this new information, and both Nikias and Isidora, Phoebe's daughter, apparently took the quiet as an invitation to make noise. They screeched as they fought over a small wooden toy, and Phoebe stepped in to mediate.

"A cross. That's how that man Jesus died? He was crucified by the Romans? What did he do to deserve that kind of death?" Anthia's rapid questions came in the order that they occurred to her. She knew that the Romans reserved crucifixion for especially heinous offenders, including runaway slaves and those who rebelled against Roman rule as traitors. "Was he a slave or a rebel?" she added.

"Neither," pronounced Eutaxia, though her next words were cut off by the arrival of Philetus and Lampo. The women all knew what that meant, and Anthia and Phoebe quickly got to their feet. Philetus commanded Nikias to come, and Anthia scooped Penelope's baby off the floor and into her arms. The baby's eyes were just as blue as his mother's, and he cooed with delight at the attention. With one hand she gestured to Demarchos, Penelope's three-year-old son, and the five of them left and walked to their room next door while Phoebe took her children and headed down the stairs. It was time to rest.

■　■　■

Anthia waited for Philetus to inform her about the morning's fishing. She knew that he didn't like too many questions, preferring to explain when he was ready. She busied herself with laying Nikias down on the mat, rubbing his back and singing quietly while sitting next to him. Her father lay on his mat in the opposing corner, breathing heavily. Her aunt paced the small space, trying to comfort Penelope's now-crying baby.

"Where are they?" she asked again, though they all knew the answer. Andrew likely wouldn't return until dusk; any chance he could find to work would be utilized. And Penelope was possibly on her way back, though depending on how far outside the city she had to go, it could be a while before she returned.

Anthia's seated posture also helped to conceal the bleeding from her husband. During the few steps between Eutaxia's one-room home and theirs Anthia had felt the blood begin again to trickle down her leg, and she quickly readjusted the rag before she sat next to her son.

"Praise be to Glaukos." Philetus's comment interrupted her thoughts. "Galleos was right; we needed to petition the fishermen's god, and Glaukos honored us with many fish this morning."

It struck Anthia that such a petition would require some coins, or at least some food. She wondered briefly where her husband and his partner had found the resources. "Yes," she agreed, "Praise be to Glaukos."

Clearly proud, Philetus pulled out from a small basket a mackerel the size of his forearm. Anthia gasped and then laughed with delight, clapping her hands. Nikias joined her in clapping, and Anthia pulled him in quickly for a hug. Her aunt stopped walking and stared, her eyes bright. But Philetus wasn't finished. Also from the basket, he drew a small amphora of wine, some cooked fava beans, and a soft loaf of bread. "We're celebrating!" declared Philetus.

Indeed, we are, thought Anthia, touching the soft bread and mentally comparing it to the flat, hard bread that she routinely baked for their family. *Finely ground flour and yeast are such wonders.*

She moved quickly, walking to Eutaxia's with her brazier to see whether there were coals she could share. During the return trip she was acutely aware of the heat of the portable appliance; carrying a full brazier, even one with handles, was an impressive feat with a pregnant belly, she decided. She carefully drizzled a bit of olive oil into the pot on top of the brazier and placed the fish inside, salting it before sealing it with the lid. While the fish cooked, she poured vinegar into the indentation on the bread plate and poured the wine into their shared cup. Knowing that there were fish to sell in the agora, Anthia gestured to the others to begin eating. They sat in their usual places on the floor around the plate and cup, tearing the bread, dipping it in vinegar, and enjoying the wine. When the fish was cooked, Anthia carefully tipped it onto

FOOD

Most of the populace in the first-century Roman Empire survived on a diet that was composed mainly of grains such as barley, wheat, and millet. Barley could be ground into flour and then combined with oil, water, or milk to make a cake called *maza*, which did not need to be baked and was often eaten by the poor. The outer hulls of barley could also be soaked overnight to soften them before grinding and cooking them as a porridge. Cheap wheat was also used for porridge and as the main ingredient in one-pound loaves of flat bread that could be made unleavened or with leavening agents such as sourdough, sour grape juice, or yeast, though bread made from quality, finely ground flour was also available.

The poor did not have separate kitchen facilities in their one-room homes, and there were no fireplaces or chimneys in these structures. The common cooking method involved the use of a brazier, a portable metal container for hot coals. Food was placed in ceramic dishes and cooked over the coals. Most people ate with their fingers and had access to plates, bowls, and cups, while the wealthy also used glassware, spoons, and knives.

Legumes (such as fava beans, field beans, peas, chickpeas, cowpeas, lupines, and lentils), vegetables, salt, olives and olive oil, vinegar, and wine (mixed with water) were also fairly common, though access to them varied greatly. The lower classes ate turnips and onions, while other vegetables and many fruits would only have been eaten occasionally (if at all). Fruits were often treated as dessert items.

Fish and meat were often reserved for the rich and special occasions, though there is some historical evidence that at least the cheaper versions were more accessible to people from the lower classes than previously thought. Fish eaten in the ancient world included octopus, sprat, sea urchins, red mullet, tuna, mussels, mackerel, and oysters. Fish were often salted so they could be eaten up to a year later. Garum—a fish sauce made by fermenting the guts of small fish (such as anchovies) with salt and herbs in large, open tanks for a month or more and then adding honey and vinegar—was popular across all socioeconomic classes of the first-century Greco-Roman world.

Meat included poultry such as ducks, geese, pigeons, owls, pelicans, swans, thrushes, larks, and nightingales as well as boar, fox, deer, and pigs. Pigs were viewed as nutritious, and they were often less expensive because of their breeding habits. The lard and blood of animals were also used; the key ingredient in black pudding was blood.

Street vendors hawked food products in urban areas, often selling breads as well as legumes and cooked meats such as sausage. Taverns, restaurants, and bars also crowded the marketplace areas and city streets. While the elite may have eaten up to three meals a day, much of the population ate when food was available to them, and that availability varied a great deal.

the plate, savoring the aroma. She smiled at Philetus, acknowledging his good work, then used her fingers to break off pieces. "What a meal!" she exalted. She felt refreshed, and it was only when she stood to walk to their stall in the agora that she remembered her bleeding. She would have to be careful to hide it from Philetus when they stopped at one of the public latrines on the way.

■　■　■

They walked down the flights of stairs and past the cesspit at the bottom, and Anthia noted that it had been emptied that morning; the mass of flies that usually covered the human excrement was a bit smaller as a result. Philetus noticed as well. "What a relief. Workers cleaned it out this morning after I left to fish with Galleos."

"Eutaxia mentioned that it was overflowing when she took the chamber pots down this morning to empty them," Anthia added, instantly scolding herself for the slip of tongue. "Pots?" asked Philetus, noticing her use of the plural. "Hers and ours," Anthia offered timidly, awaiting the scolding that she knew would come.

"Why is she doing your work? You shame our family when you do not work hard and complete your tasks."

"I wasn't feeling well, so she offered to help me. I am feeling better now." Anthia paused, wondering whether her careful comment would be enough to satisfy him.

"That was honorable of her. I must thank Lampo when I see him next."

Anthia breathed a sigh of relief and made a mental note to mention it to Eutaxia first. A few minutes later they arrived at the latrine and entered the dim room as a family. They took three seats in a row, and Anthia was grateful that the poor light helped to hide her bleeding. Just to be sure, she helped Nikias first, hoisting his naked little body up to the seat, and waited to sit until Philetus leaned forward to select a sponge stick that he would use to clean himself when he was finished. She sat quickly, her arm touching her son's. She waited to rise until Philetus had walked to the water basin to rinse his hands, quickly adjusting the rag and her tunic. *I wish we could use the baths next door*, she thought.

As if he had heard her thoughts, Philetus turned to her, "Perhaps we can visit the baths today after we sell our fish in the agora. If we sell them all, we should be able to pay the fee."

She smiled gratefully and nodded. "That would be wonderful."

URBAN SANITATION

Sanitation in the ancient world often involved cesspits (which could be many feet deep) in courtyards and on streets. Very few homes had running water or private toilets, so ceramic chamber pots were used and then dumped into cesspits or onto the street. People sometimes relieved themselves on public streets, which could be covered not just with human excrement but with animal manure, mud, and even corpses. Such unsanitary conditions attracted flies and other insects that also encouraged the spread of disease.

In major cities the multiseated public latrine was fairly common, though single toilets were also constructed in shops and bars. Seats were a mere twelve inches apart without partitions in between them.

Latrines were often connected to a bathhouse so that water from the bath could be used to flush out the sewage under the seats of the latrine.

Some public latrines added a narrow gutter of shallow water in the center of the room, which likely was provided to rinse out a sponge stick after cleaning the anus with it. Sometimes basins of water were placed for the purpose of rinsing hands, but there was no soap or towels.

Figure 2.3. Public toilets. Very few ancient homes had private toilets

They walked toward the agora, and from a distance Anthia could see the crowd gathered outside Tyrannus's lecture hall. "That philosopher Paul is really starting to cause a ruckus." Philetus shook his head emphatically. "Something needs to be done. Surely one of our great Ephesian philosophers can best him in public debate and quiet things down."

"Yes, surely," Anthia agreed, though she thought it likely that some had already tried. As they walked behind the crowd, Anthia strained her ears to listen.

" . . . the true lord," the now-familiar voice of Paul argued.

"Caesar is lord!" a contrarian voice insisted. "This is obvious to anyone with eyes to see. Look at the might and expanse of the Roman empire."

The tone of Paul's response caught Anthia's attention, though she missed the end of the sentence because she could no longer hear. "Sometimes our eyes cannot see what is true. The one true god of the world has seated Jesus at his right hand in the heavenly realms. Jesus is lord over . . ." As Eutaxia had explained, Paul didn't sound angry or superior. He sounded . . . excited. Joyful.

Hmm, Anthia pondered as she struggled to keep up with her husband's quick strides while not losing the rag that was placed so precariously between her legs. *I wonder how long it will take the authorities to do something about Paul and his claims that someone besides Caesar or one of the gods is lord.*

They walked to their fish stall and were greeted by others in their fishers and fishmongers' association, including their wives and children. The men divided up some of the fish among themselves and left with the older boys to trade for other necessities. This was an important part of the boys' training, as they would be fishermen as well someday.

The rest of the afternoon was a blur of bargaining, selling, and trading the many fish the men had caught. The women always managed this aspect of the work, along with keeping an eye on the children. Thankfully, a couple of the families who shared the fish stall had older girls who managed the younger children. Anthia spotted Dorema, the six-year-old daughter of Galleos and his wife, Euippe, chasing after Nikias. She caught him and swung his little body up into her arms, laughing. *Dorema. Gift.* The pang of grief for her friend swelled, and Anthia wondered whether Philetus would accept a suggestion of a name for their unborn baby. *Dorema would be appropriate*, she argued to herself. *And if it is a boy, then Diodorus. Gift of Zeus.*

The men returned, congratulating each other on their abilities to trade well. Philetus instructed her to find Nikias so they could visit the baths, and Anthia quickly obliged. She found him on Dorema's hip, the girl's left hand wrapped around him. On their way to the baths they again passed in front of the stall where she had seen Paul yesterday. He wasn't there, though the other man and woman were busy sewing what appeared to be a tent, or possibly a sun shade. The reason for his absence in the stall became apparent as they walked past the lecture hall, for Paul's audience had only grown in the intervening hours. The topic was unchanged, and Anthia heard bits of what was being said. Paul was saying something about the authority of lords, including how they demonstrated their rule over their subjects. The rule of Jesus was, apparently, different. Anthia was interested, wishing she could stay to hear more. But Philetus was undeterred, moving quickly toward the baths, and Anthia followed. She was relieved that she wasn't currently bleeding; otherwise the baths could be awkward.

As she settled into the hot water, she mentally thanked the Romans for their love of bathing and their skill in designing furnaces that could heat water to this temperature. She and Philetus had undressed in the *apodyterium*, where their clothes were stored and watched by an attendant, and they had moved quickly through the tepid water in the transitional room to the hot water here in the *caldarium*. She was sitting next to Philetus with Nikias on her lap, though they were not alone. On her other side sat two men who were clearly discussing some kind of business deal that involved olives. Across the room a woman was being washed with soap by her young slave girl. Two young men entered, red-faced from their exercise in the *palaestra* outside. There were almost always men—and sometimes women—in that courtyard who were running, wrestling, or lifting weights. Even the thought of exercising was draining to Anthia. *Running would make me even hungrier than I already am.*

She had been concerned about leaving their clothes in the *apodyterium*; she and Philetus each had only one tunic, and she had heard that clothes had been stolen from this bath in recent days. As she prayed that the gods would guard her clothes, she appraised the young men, who were taking their time getting into the communal bathing pool. They were young and muscular, and the way they strutted and preened suggested a confidence bolstered by high status. She could tell by their shiny skin that they had visited the masseuse first. Most of the oil from the massage had been scraped off with a strigil, but they still glistened in the afternoon heat. They finally sat down, each with a depilator, who proceeded to pluck their underarm hair while they talked.

Anthia turned her head and noticed several older women sitting on Philetus's other side, their wealth apparent because of their plump bodies. They were chatting while eating chicken legs they had no doubt purchased from the street vendor outside. *Smells delicious*, was Anthia's first thought, though it was followed quickly by another when she heard one of them mention

the name Paul. *Is it the Paul from the lecture hall?* Anthia wondered. She listened carefully, trying to tune out the other conversations in the room so she could focus on what the older
women were saying.

"Yes, he is," one of them remarked. "Dorcas insisted on paying
the rent for the lecture hall. I told her that it was unwise, as he
is creating quite a stir, but she wouldn't listen to me. Even her
husband refutes Paul's claims, but she has her own inheritance,
and she is paying the rent out of those funds."

This woman knows the master that Eutaxia heard earlier!
Anthia watched her husband out of the corner of her eye, looking
for an indication that he was listening, but he seemed lost in his
own thoughts. *Useless,* she decided after several minutes of
eavesdropping. *They aren't talking about what Paul is saying,
they're just discussing the risks their friend is taking by helping
Paul.* She had sometimes seen women who spoke in public be
ridiculed, but wealthy women like Dorcas were often educated
and trained in various arts.

Philetus handed her a bit of the soap for which he had traded
that afternoon, and she quickly worked to scrub herself and
Nikias. While washing her belly she pushed in several places,
waiting for the baby's kick to answer her. *Nothing,* she worried.
At least she was not bleeding at the moment, a small comfort.
When they finished, they stood and walked to the final room, the
frigidarium. As Anthia plunged under the cold water, her shiver
was met with a kick, and she praised Artemis for her care.

■   ■   ■

Their dinner that night was a celebration. *Two good meals
in one day!* Anthia rejoiced. She looked around Galleos and
Euippe's home, surveying the gathering. Several of the families in their association had decided to eat and honor Glaukos

together, and Galleos's home had been the obvious choice for the gathering. *Two small rooms gives more space than one, after all.*

Anthia watched as one of the men poured wine out of a cup onto a small altar in the corner of one of the rooms. A chorus of "Praise be to Glaukos" reverberated throughout the space, and several voices added their own prayers of thanks to the god for hearing them earlier. Euippe's mention of the god as "lord Glaukos" caught Anthia's attention, reminding her of Paul's comments earlier in the lecture hall. *Paul would say that Jesus is lord, not Glaukos.* The unbidden thought caught her off-guard, and she scanned the room to see whether anyone could sense her shameful thoughts. *No one knows,* she told herself. *Unless . . . does Glaukos know?* Anthia wasn't sure how far Glaukos's reach extended, and her ignorance scared her. "Praise be to Glaukos!" she called out, and the entire group turned at the volume of her response. "Praise be to Glaukos!" they affirmed, and Anthia exhaled, hoping that all was well.

Day 3, Friday

DAY OF VENUS/APHRODITE

◆

THE POUNDING ON THE DOOR WAS LOUD. Very loud. Anthia was awake and had been for some time, but she touched her husband to wake him. "Philetus." He blinked and rose, walking the few steps to the door. It opened to Lampo's anxious face.

"Euxinus has a fever." His pronouncement stole Anthia's breath, and she looked to Philetus for a response.

"What do you need?"

"I am going to petition Asclepius, the god of healing, on behalf of my son. He is weak, and we are afraid to move him. Will you send Anthia to petition Artemis, our great protector?" He pressed a small bag of grain into Philetus's hand.

"Of course," Philetus replied. "We will help." Lampo left, and Philetus picked up a piece of bread and a few figs. "I will be with Galleos and a few others again today. Do what you can to help my cousin and Eutaxia, and I will be back midday." He dropped the grain into her outstretched hands and left.

Anthia looked around the room, noting her aunt's worried face and her father's exhausted stare. As usual, Andrew had left in the predawn darkness to advertise his labor in the agora. That left her and Penelope, but between them they had a pregnant belly and three children.

When she was sure that Philetus was gone, she stood up to use the chamber pot. She inspected it afterwards, noting the blood in her urine. *I cannot think about that right now. Eutaxia needs me.* She packed a few pieces of bread and two figs for herself and Nikias, then glanced at Penelope.

Penelope bound her baby to her chest, talking while she did so. "Today I'll take him. I know exactly where I'm going, and it's nearby. I talked with a farmer's wife yesterday just outside the city whose husband will be busy all day selling their harvest at the agora. She will allow me to glean from the leftovers in the field. I'll also take Demarchos," she said, gesturing for her three-year-old to join her. "He can be helpful today and work alongside me." Anthia nodded silently, and Penelope was gone.

She grabbed Nikias's hand and walked next door.

She knocked softly and entered without waiting for a response. Eutaxia's worried face looked up from her place on the floor, where she was sitting next to her son's prostrate body. "He's burning up. It started several hours ago and has only gotten worse." She shook her head. "I don't know what else to do." Anthia wanted to hug her friend, but her fear for her own son's health kept her at the door.

"I'm going to help. Nikias and I will go to the Artemesion." She forced herself to project confidence. "He'll be fine. I know it." Eutaxia smiled weakly and nodded.

Anthia marched quickly down the stairs and out into the street. Nikias complained at her tight grip, but she shushed him impatiently. She wanted to run, but her belly made it impossible. She settled for walking quickly, half-dragging Nikias at her side. Willing herself not to cry, she focused on her destination, ignoring the busyness of the street and the smells of food, animals, and sewage. Suddenly an imperial statue caught her eye. *Caesar. Claudius. Could you help us? You've filled our city with your likeness; would you stoop to save a child who is his father's only heir?* Her heart pounded in fear as her thoughts raced. *Euxinus looked terrible, even from across the room. . . . What will Euxaxia do if she loses another child? . . . What caused his sickness? Is one of the gods angry with Eutaxia or Lampo? . . . What if Nikias becomes ill as well?* Suddenly the Artemision loomed before her, its imposing size, as usual, making her feel small and unworthy. She walked quickly past famous sculptures and paintings, heading straight for the area where the priestesses often spent time. A woman was there, prostrate in prayer, though she rose and listened to Anthia's anxious story. She accepted the small bag of grain and promised to offer incense to Artemis, asking for the goddess to spare the life of Euxinus.

Anthia didn't stay to watch the process; she rushed back, stopping only at a fountain to get a drink of water for herself and Nikias. From the top of the stairs in the *insula* she could see that Eutaxia's door was open, and the reason became clear as she got

Figure 3.1. An artist's rendering of the temple of Artemis

MEDICINE AND PHYSICIANS

Physicians in the ancient world were mostly male, while midwives were female. First- and second-century Ephesus boasted two famous male doctors, though only the wealthy elite could afford such services. There was a lot of misunderstanding about the human body, and medicines and treatments often contained elements of folklore. The poor, who couldn't afford the services of physicians, often resorted to folk healers, herbalists, and snake charmers. Known medicines involved vegetables such as cabbage, herbs such as dill and cumin, and ointments of sulfide, myrrh, and copper oxides.

Because of the limited treatments offered by physicians, people from all classes and status levels sought help at the shrines of healing gods such as Asclepius, the patron god of physicians. He was called "Savior" by his devotees, and his famous symbol of intertwined snakes on a staff is known even today. Some of his shrines had been built up into large complexes, with spaces for treatment, libraries, baths, and latrines. Patients sometimes slept at these shrines, awaiting a dream from Asclepius, which would be interpreted by priests.

closer. *Zotike.* Eutaxia's sister Zotike had also been part of Anthia's childhood, though she was several years older.

Zotike stood up and met her in the doorway. "Stay here. Keep Nikias away from Euxinus." Anthia assumed that Philetus had sent Zotike, and Zotike confirmed it. "Philetus stopped by this morning on his way to the temple of Asclepius. He asked me to visit my sister and nephew today, and to pray to the gods—many gods—with him." She paused. "Euxinus's fever is so high . . . I don't think I've ever touched skin that is so hot."

Zotike got out a small pouch, then turned and walked to where Euxinus lay. She removed a pinch of something that appeared to be a dried herb and inserted it into her nephew's mouth. Anthia watched from the doorway, afraid to enter.

"Can I bring some water?" she asked, desperate to be given a meaningful task that would take her and Nikias away from the room.

"Yes!" Zotike barked urgently. "Will you take your own jar to the fountain? Eutaxia's is filled with rags that we are using to try to cool his skin. He needs water to drink, if we can get him to do it." Anthia fled from the doorway to her own home, breathing heavily. Nikias whined and asked to go back and play.

I wonder if I have time to take him to Phoebe's, she thought desperately. *Anything to get him away from this sickness.* She lifted their water jar and walked to the stairs, dragging Nikias past his friend's door. "No, Nikias! Not today!" Her heart sank even as she added the words, "Maybe tomorrow." She knew the situation was dire.

As she walked to the fountain she considered her options again. Should she go straight to the fountain, or did she have time to take Nikias to Phoebe's first? It wasn't that far away, though it would take several minutes to walk there.

"Dorema!" a mother called nearby, "Come here!" The mention of her friend's name stopped her in her tracks, and she watched the young child run to her mother, her dark hair unbound and bouncing with each step.

Too much death, she thought angrily. *No more. I'm taking him to Phoebe's.*

■　■　■

Phoebe opened the door with a smile that froze the instant she saw Anthia's face. Her curly hair was even wilder today than usual, and her olive skin shimmered with perspiration. Her baby was tied to her back, sleeping. "What is it? Your bleeding? The baby?" She reached for Anthia's arms and pulled her into a hug. "Tell me."

Anthia broke down and cried. Between sobs she gasped, "I'm still bleeding. I don't know what to do. And now Euxinus is sick. His fever is so high, he's burning up. I'm afraid for Nikias."

TEXTILES

Working with textiles was a common occupation in the ancient world. Guilds of clothiers, linen workers, wool merchants, and dyers all participated in the textile production process. Wool work, often done by women, was also portrayed symbolically throughout the Greco-Roman world as the appropriate activity of a virtuous woman in the home. Because wool, goat hair, and linen were used not only for clothing but for sails, tents, and sun awnings, the materials were in high demand.

Figure 3.2. A distaff used for spinning wool. Working with textiles was a common occupation in the ancient world

The stages of the process employed many people. Sheep and goats were raised for their wool and hair, as were plants such as flax for their fibers. These materials were often dyed as part of the process of production for the wealthy, though much of the population would have worn simple clothing that was made from undyed wool. For at least some of the population in the first century, linen (rather than wool) undergarments were the new standard.

Wool needed to be spun, and women would place raw wool on a distaff and hold it, often under an arm. The other arm was used for spinning the fibers, creating thread that was wound onto a spindle. Women would often prop their feet onto a stool and use a protective covering over their clothing to protect it from being stained by grease and dirt. After spinning, the thread or yarn was woven into fabric on a loom, and then it could be used to make clothing and other products.

Figure 3.3. A Roman loom. After spinning, thread or yarn was woven into fabric on a loom and then used to make clothing and other products

Tarsus, the apostle Paul's hometown, was famous for linen weavers and the use of Cilician goat hair for making tents that were exceptionally heat- and water-resistant. Ephesus was noted for its towel weavers, who had organized themselves into a guild for their mutual benefit and prosperity.

Phoebe nodded calmly. "I'll keep Nikias, of course." She glanced toward where he was already playing with her daughter. "Isidora will be thrilled if he stays, even overnight." She paused, then gestured around the room, where several of her female relatives, including her mother-in-law, sister-in-law, and two nieces were sitting with their distaffs or looms, spinning or weaving wool. Most of the wool they were using had already been dyed; there was red, blue, and even purple. Clearly there was a contract in play with a wealthy family or perhaps a nearby clothier. Anthia noted—not for the first time—that the grim look Phoebe's mother-in-law wore was matched by the way she pulled her hair tightly into the roll at the back of her neck. The woman intimidated her, and Anthia took a step back involuntarily. "One of my nieces will watch him," Phoebe added. "I have work to do, but it should be fine."

"Thank you." Anthia composed herself and straightened her shoulders. "I have to go. Eutaxia and Zotike need water, and I told them I'd get it."

"Go," Phoebe said, waving her hand for emphasis. "We're fine here."

Anthia could feel the sweat dropping down into her *strophium*, the band of cloth encircling her chest, as she carried the jar to the fountain. *I wish it was winter*, she thought briefly. From the moment she got pregnant she had been hot—always hot—and the weather just made her more uncomfortable. She noticed a little naked boy playing in a puddle. *Enjoy it now*, she counseled silently. *In just a year or two you will be working alongside the rest of your family.*

At the fountain she was obliged to sit to fill her jug. She immersed her hands and arms in the cool water as she filled the jug, savoring the relief it offered. She lifted it to her belly and rested it on the top, balancing it with her hands. She knew from experience that she couldn't hold it out in front of her without support. Usually the baby kicked when she constricted his space like this, but today there was no response. All she could feel was the dull pain in her abdomen that had started with the bleeding. She prayed again to Artemis as she walked. A glance upward revealed another imperial statue, and Anthia offered a prayer to Caesar as well. *Who will help?* she wondered.

. . .

Anthia heard Lampo's voice before she saw him. "I was sure that Asclepius or Artemis would hear my request and respond! We used the last of our grain for the sacrificial incense and libations! How can his fever be worse?" The anger in his voice was mixed with anguish. She carried the water jug to the women and set it down. Feeling helpless, she backed up and stood against the wall.

Zotike spoke slowly. "There is one other thing we could try."

Lampo considered his son's listless body before answering. "What is it? And why haven't you brought it up before now?" In response Zotike reached for a wet rag. She folded it and placed it on her nephew's forehead. Impatient, Lampo's voice increased in volume. "What, woman? Tell me."

"There is a man named Paul who teaches in the lecture hall of Tyrannus near the Tetragonos Agora," she began.

Anthia's ears roared. *Paul again! But how could a teacher help?* She focused her attention when she realized that Zotike was still talking.

" . . . named Jesus who is the ultimate healer. He is a worshiper of this Jesus and can heal in his name. I heard a story from a woman at the water fountain yesterday; she said that she had been bleeding for years, but when her son brought her an apron that Paul had touched, it healed her."

Lampo's surprise was palpable. "Why haven't I heard of Paul if he is such a great healer?"

"He is a Jew who only recently came to Ephesus," Zotike answered. "At first he only taught in the Jewish synagogue, but now he is teaching publicly for all who wish to hear."

Lampo pondered this new information, and Anthia silently wondered how much information Zotike possessed. *She must know more than she's saying. Perhaps I should speak up? . . . No, I do not have answers, just questions.*

She was still waffling when Lampo spoke. "A Jew? So this is a Jewish god?" Zotike's nod was his only answer. "Do we risk offending our gods by petitioning this Jewish god as well?"

"If we do not take that risk, Euxinus may die," Zotike affirmed.

"I will go to find this man Paul," Lampo decided.

■   ■   ■

Anthia, Eutaxia, and Zotike waited in the hot room. *She's really worried*, thought Anthia, noting her friend's quiet mood. *Normally she's so talkative.* There really wasn't enough for all three of them to do, but none of them was willing to leave the support of their small sisterhood in that moment. There was also the question of Paul's help, and Anthia was curious to hear of Lampo's visit.

"It is time to rest and eat a few bites," Zotike announced.

"I am not hungry," came Eutaxia's whispered response, and Anthia added her agreement.

"You don't get a choice," Zotike stated flatly, and Anthia tried not to smile at the way it reminded her of Eutaxia.

Eutaxia when she's not in crisis, anyway, she considered. She took the piece of flat cake offered by Zotike and was surprised when Zotike grabbed her arm as well.

"Go home and lie down for a while," she ordered, spinning her to face the door. "Eutaxia told me about the bleeding. We'll be

fine here while we wait for Lampo. I need to help Eutaxia get
some mending done anyway; some customers are expecting it."

Anthia obeyed, feeling relieved. She knew that her body could
use the rest, and besides, she would hear when Lampo returned.
She walked next door, and even in those few steps, she could feel
the wetness on her thighs. Once inside, she surveyed the still
forms of her father and aunt. *I'm glad they're sleeping.* Andrew
and Penelope were both still out, as she had expected. She
turned her back to the sleeping forms and quickly inspected the
rag, washed herself, and put a clean rag in place. She lay down
on the mat and savored the relief it gave to her back and feet. She
listened to the noises of her neighbors—babies crying, voices
arguing, someone singing, metal clicking—there was never a
quiet moment here. The ache in her belly was still there, and she
massaged her skin with both hands while she waited for the baby
to kick back. Nothing happened. She rubbed more vigorously,
intent on jarring him into action. Still nothing. *Come on, baby,
come on, baby.* She matched the rhythm of her words to the
movement of her hands, hoping for some response. After a while
her arms ached, and she stopped. Then a new fear occurred to
her. *If my baby is dead, I will still have to give birth to him. How
will I have the strength?* She began praying to Artemis, then
Asclepius. She wondered whether she should pray to Paul, or
perhaps the Jesus he had mentioned. *Jesus,* she began hesitat-
ingly. *Save the son in my belly. Please.*

.   .   .

She must have dozed, because Lampo's voice startled her into
consciousness. "I have it, I have it!" he was exclaiming triumphantly.

Anthia rose quickly, eager to see what Lampo had brought
with him and hear the details of the encounter. She wanted to
walk over immediately, but she needed to use the chamber pot

first. *Everything is squished in there*, she reflected, squatting uncomfortably. *I feel like I'm always needing the chamber pot or the latrine.* She noted the lack of bleeding and silently rejoiced, then stood to adjust the cloth wrapped around her hips and between her legs. *Ow!* she exclaimed, touching her left rib cage where a strong kick had jarred her. *That was a big one.* Her initial excitement wavered as she remembered what she had done prior to her nap. *I prayed to Jesus. Did he cause my son to kick, or was it Artemis?* Fear gripped her, but she told herself not to focus on it. *Not now. Now is about Euxinus.*

No one looked up as she entered; they were all examining a small piece of cloth. "What is that?" Anthia asked in puzzlement.

They hesitated, and finally Lampo spoke. "A handkerchief that Paul has touched."

Anthia shivered as she walked closer to see for herself. "Looks like a typical rag or small towel. Do you think it could actually work? And where did you get it?" She knew, of course, that items like this could mediate the power of a god, but she had never seen it for herself.

Lampo adjusted his sandal strap and tilted his head as he looked at her. His dark eyes were bright and clear. "From Paul. I found him near the lecture hall, as Zotike said I would. He was surrounded by a crowd—a mob, really—and it took me a while to edge my way up to him. When I was finally close enough, I told him about Euxinus. I begged him to heal our son and told him that while I couldn't pay him, I would be willing to trade services at our fullery if he needed anything laundered." Lampo shook his head in disbelief. "Paul didn't want money. He said that he isn't healing in his own power; he is healing in the name of a man named Jesus, and Jesus heals as a demonstration of the kind of lord he is. He is a ruler who heals and restores; those are the priorities of his kingdom. I told him that I'd never heard of a lord who didn't want something in return, and Paul laughed at me. Laughed! He said, 'Oh yes, Lampo, he does want something in return. You. Your loyalty and commitment to honor him and no other lords. But you can choose whether you want to do that. It's up to you.'"

"Wait." Eutaxia looked at each of them in turn, filtering her thoughts as she prepared to speak. "So this Jesus will heal to demonstrate who he is and how much power he has, and he wants our loyalty in return, but he doesn't require it to heal? I don't understand this god. It doesn't make sense."

"We can discuss that later," Zotike stated flatly. "When did he give you the handkerchief? And did he tell you how to use it? Do we need to say anything? An incantation of some kind, perhaps where we repeat Jesus' name again and again? A prayer?"

Lampo again shook his head. "He told me that he wished he could come to see Euxinus and pray for him in the name of Jesus, but there were so many others in the crowd who were waiting to speak with him. He handed me this handkerchief and told me to touch Euxinus with it. Then . . ." Lampo hesitated, clearing his throat.

"Then, what?" demanded Zotike. "If there are further instructions, we need to know."

"No, it's not that," Lampo clarified. "After giving me the handkerchief, Paul clasped me by the shoulders and kissed me on the cheek. 'Until next time, brother,' he said." The group stood in silence while they considered this.

Finally, Eutaxia spoke up. "We can discuss Paul later. Let's see if this works." She took the handkerchief and laid it out carefully on Euxinus's chest. Anthia noted his shallow breathing, realizing she was holding her own breath. They watched and waited.

"How long—" Zotike's question was interrupted by Euxinus, who raised his arm and rubbed his eye. Startled, they all watched to see what he would do next. He opened his eyes and sat up, yawning. He seemed confused by the four adult faces that were looking so intently at him, but his first priority was clear. "I thirsty. My tummy hungry." He raised his eyebrows hopefully, glancing from one face to the next.

Anthia felt faint. She sat down—too quickly, she realized, as her hand and right thigh bumped hard on the floor. Eutaxia paused only for a moment, answering quickly while touching Euxinus's forehead with her hand. "Of course, my son. Would you like some water and bread?" She looked around the room and mouthed "fever gone" while she stood, and Lampo knelt to see for himself.

"You aren't hot," he murmured, almost to himself.

"No, Daddy, not hot. Hungry. Hungry." Euxinus corrected. "What this?" he continued, picking up the handkerchief that had fallen into his lap as he sat.

Lampo's laughter answered him. "That, my son, is a miracle."

Clearly uninterested in his father's explanation, Euxinus stood and ran to his mother's legs, chanting "hungry, hungry." She handed him a cup of water and a piece of bread, and he greedily accepted her offerings.

Eutaxia's smile radiated through the room as she turned to Zotike and Anthia. "He's well! Thank the gods!"

Lampo corrected her gently. "No, Eutaxia, thank Jesus."

Eutaxia pursed her lips then nodded. "Yes, thank Jesus. He healed my son." She began to jump up and down, laughing and crying. Her celebration was contagious, and Anthia found herself joining her friend, though her belly required lower jumps. *I've never seen Eutaxia like this*, she thought. Zotike was next, and finally even Lampo joined in, his bellowing laughter filling the small room. The banging of the door caused all of them to turn. Philetus was standing in the doorway with a confused look on his face.

"Philetus!" Lampo enjoined. "There you are, my cousin!"

Bewildered, Philetus answered. "I'm sorry for returning so late. I meant to come earlier, but Galleos and I were having great luck while fishing." He hesitated, looking at the faces of Anthia, Lampo, Eutaxia, and Zotike. His gaze finally shifted behind them, to where Euxinus was stuffing the last bit of bread into his mouth. Philetus's mouth gaped when Euxinus gulped the last of his water and burped loudly. "What . . ." he began.

"He's healed, Philetus." Eutaxia's declaration clearly didn't satisfy Philetus, who persisted.

"How was he healed? Which god restored him? Was it Asclepius? Or Artemis?"

The group glanced at each other and finally Lampo spoke. "Have you heard of the man named Paul who teaches and dialogues in the lecture hall of Tyrannus?" The question clearly surprised Philetus, but he nodded. "It was his god, the one named Jesus, who healed Euxinus."

"But . . . how?" was all that Philetus could muster. "Isn't he Jewish?"

This time Eutaxia spoke. "Zotike met a woman at the fountain who was healed by an apron that Paul had touched. Artemis and Asclepius were not responding—apparently they were not pleased with our petitions—and Euxinus was only declining. We decided it was worth a try."

"But how did you find a handkerchief that Paul had touched? And why would Paul heal a non-Jew?" Philetus was clearly finding his bearings; the relevant questions were finally coming.

Lampo stepped forward as he began to talk. "I went to find him. I waited with a crowd near the lecture hall until I was close enough to talk with him. He didn't even ask if I was Jewish, he just listened while I told him about Euxinus. Then he gave me this handkerchief and called me 'brother.'"

"But—but I thought Jesus was a man, not a god," Philetus said. "When I heard Paul talking with someone else a couple of days ago, that's what it sounded like."

"He didn't say anything about that, and I didn't ask. But . . ." Lampo thought for a moment. "That would be like our emperors, who are also both human and divine." He smiled a bit, looking satisfied with this solution. "The most important part is that it worked," he added. "Look at my son!" The adults all turned to look, and Euxinus sensed the sets of eyes on him, freezing in place. A small piece of bread was hanging out of his mouth.

"Euxinus!" exclaimed Eutaxia. "That bread was for dinner!" But then she laughed. She picked him up, kissing his face and laughing.

"Well . . . this is cause for a celebration!" proclaimed Philetus. "Our catch of fish today was massive. Anthia, it's time to come to the fish stall and sell them. Tonight we'll celebrate."

.   .   .

As they walked to Phoebe's, Anthia marveled at Euxinus's health. "Did you see him eat, Philetus?"

"I couldn't miss it," Philetus answered with a smile.

"He seems to be in even better health than before he got sick!"

"Maybe Lampo will indeed have a son carry on his name," Philetus added. "When their other babies died shortly after birth, and then when Euxinus survived but was so weak, I wondered if Lampo's line would end with him. It appears not."

They passed another statue of the emperor, and Anthia pondered again the idea that Jesus could be both human and divine.

Suddenly, a cry of "Mama!" interrupted her reverie. She scanned the area ahead for the face of her son and found him near Phoebe's daughter Isidora in the street. One of Phoebe's nieces was with them. "Hello, Basilissa," she greeted the eight-year-old. "Thank you for watching him." The girl nodded shyly, glancing sideways at Philetus. "May I speak briefly with Phoebe?" Anthia asked her husband. "I would like to tell her about Euxinus and invite their family to the celebration." Philetus grunted his approval, pointing toward the public latrines nearby. He walked toward them, and Anthia scooped up Euxinus and walked to her friend's apartment.

As she knocked she could hear the chatter of women, and when another niece opened the door, Anthia could see the women busily working. "Anthia!" called Phoebe, quickly standing and leaving her loom to walk toward the door. As she walked, she adjusted her baby, who was nursing while wrapped in a sling around her chest. Her worried eyes searched Anthia's face.

"Tell me," she demanded. "Has something happened to Euxinus?"

In that moment Anthia realized that her friend assumed the worst; why else would she have returned so quickly? She decided to be direct. "He's healed. He's fine, and healthy, and eating and drinking nonstop."

Phoebe's surprise was apparent. "Asclepius? Artemis?"

Anthia shook her head. "No, Jesus. The one the man Paul, who teaches in the lecture hall, worships." Anthia knew her friend had many questions, but she also knew there were many fish to sell. "Come tonight to eat dinner with us and Lampo and Eutaxia. We are going to celebrate Euxinus's health. And I'll tell you the whole story then. I need to go now and sell fish."

Her friend's eyes signaled both understanding and impatience. "Fine, then," Phoebe said. "I suppose I'll have to wait. I'll send a few of the older children to tell my husband."

Philetus walked up and gestured impatiently, and Anthia picked up Nikias, who squirmed unhappily in her arms.

Anthia set him down as they walked to the agora, grabbing his hand instead. *I just can't carry him with my big belly*, she thought for the hundredth time. *There's no room for him.* She used her free hand to push on her belly while she walked, again trying to provoke a response from within. Nothing. She wondered again about the power of Jesus. *Could he save my baby? Would he? Does it matter that I am not Jewish? It did not matter for Euxinus. Perhaps . . . ?*

Her musing was interrupted by shouts coming from a crowd up ahead. Philetus was also curious, and he quickened his already-brisk pace to see what was happening. As they grew closer, Anthia could see a man being restrained by several other men. He was clearly trying to get away, and it looked almost like a wrestling match. Suddenly the man growled. His back arched and contorted in what looked to be a humanly impossible way, and one by one he picked up the men restraining him and threw them to the ground. Anthia gasped along with the crowd, which grew silent when the man spoke. "My name is Legion," he declared.

A woman near Anthia whispered to the woman next to her, "It is the demon again. That is not my husband Philip. That is not his voice. It's the demon's voice." She was holding a small piece of cloth in her hand, and in a flash Anthia realized what was happening. The woman nodded at the group of men, who leaped together on the man in the next moment.

As they did, the woman ran forward and covered her husband's head with the handkerchief. What started as another growl grew and morphed into a screech. The crowd watched in stunned silence as he hunched into a fetal position, his body rolling in wave-like movements. The men holding him moved away one by one until he was alone. He began speaking in a language that Anthia did not understand, but then she caught a word that she knew. He screamed it, extending the sound for several seconds.

"JEEEEESUUUUS!"

Anthia felt as if she'd been slapped. She grabbed for Philetus's hand, feeling faint for the second time that day. She watched as the man slumped, his body relaxing. He lay on the ground quietly, as if sleeping. Suddenly his eyes opened, and he sat up. His posture was expectant, and it reminded Anthia of Euxinus earlier.

The next question only encouraged the comparison, for the man stated, in a different voice than he had used earlier, "I'm thirsty. May I have some water?"

The crowd was electrified by this statement, and everyone began talking at once. Except Anthia. She watched as the woman who had placed the cloth on her husband's head ran forward and embraced him, weeping. He hugged her back, weeping along with her. A couple of young men broke free from the crowd and joined them, crying and laughing. The scene was reminiscent of the one that Anthia had participated in earlier that day, and the parallel struck her to her core.

"Jesus," she breathed. "Your power is truly enormous." She wanted to continue watching them, but when Philetus touched her shoulder and pointed toward the agora, she nodded in agreement. They had work to do.

They walked quietly toward their fish stall, each processing what they had just seen. "Did you hear what the man said?" questioned Philetus.

"Yes," she answered, then paused, almost afraid to say it out loud. "Jesus."

Philetus shook his head in confusion. "What is happening? And what of Artemis and her honor? She will not appreciate another god usurping her role as protector and savior of Ephesus. She is the one who keeps us healthy."

Anthia felt the tension as well. *This cannot end well*, she thought silently.

■　■　■

The rest of the afternoon was a blur of haggling, trading, and selling. Anthia's proudest moment had been when she sold one large mackerel for a denarius. *A day's wage!* she celebrated inwardly. *That woman must have been in a hurry, or perhaps she's so wealthy that the price doesn't matter.* The catch was indeed huge, but the agora was filled with people. The crowds were also talking about what had just happened outside the agora in the street. *News sure travels fast,* Anthia noted, when the third person in a row asked her about it. "Yes, I was there," she confirmed, telling the story again.

"I heard," her customer added, "that a little boy was healed this morning through another handkerchief touched by Paul. Do you know anything about that?" Anthia hesitated, wondering how much to share. The look on her face must have given it away, because the woman pressed her with another question. "Were you present for that one as well? Tell me, is it true?" Anthia glanced to her right, noticing that a couple of the other wives whose husbands were fishermen in their association were listening as well.

"Um . . ." began Anthia. Her mind worked frantically, trying to decide how much was safe to tell. She was beginning to think that her presence at the two healings was unfortunate. *Will this make me a target of Artemis's anger?* she wondered? *Will she refuse to save my baby because of this?*

A new customer pushed her way up to the counter and interrupted, granting Anthia a reprieve. "Will you trade one of those tuna for some barley flour and olive oil?" she asked, pointing to the row of hanging fish.

"It's possible," Anthia replied. "How much flour and oil?"

The women settled the transaction, and Anthia turned back to the woman who was still waiting for an answer. She hesitated again when she felt a trickle of blood moving down her thigh.

Artemis, she reminded herself silently. "I don't know," she told the woman. "I wasn't there." Her heart pounded in her chest as she waited for the woman's response. Thankfully, the woman turned and left.

■ ■ ■

Anthia enjoyed the steam rising from the hot water. *What a treat. Two days in a row*, she celebrated silently. She lifted Nikias's leg from the water so that she could inspect his legs and feet. "Dirty," she declared, "especially the bottom. Were you playing in mud this morning at Phoebe's?" Anthia wished that they could afford leather sandals for him, but he grew so quickly that it didn't make sense to spend so much on an item of luxury.

Today the bath was full; there were many more people than yesterday, including more children and women. The water was moving and churning as children swam and adults climbed in and out. Anthia smiled at the young woman next to her, who also

Figure 3.4. A bathhouse in Ephesus

had a big belly, and the woman smiled back. She leaned back and listened to the chatter and noises as she planned her contributions for the celebration that evening. *Let's see . . . I need to make some* maza *cakes, now that I have some barley flour and olive oil.* She could buy bread, as the fish had sold well that afternoon, but she had decided to put the money toward a different kind of treat. *Pork.* She could hardly wait to taste the pork sausages she and Philetus had purchased from a vendor. The bite that Eutaxia had shared yesterday only increased her craving. Philetus had also traded fish for a few onions and turnips, and those needed to be cooked. *That shouldn't take too long,* she told herself. *We have plenty of time to finish that before the others come.* She checked on Nikias—he was still near her, splashing—and then arched her back in an attempt to stretch the front side of her body. A sharp pain hit her in the belly as she moved, and she tensed and froze as she processed it. She glanced down at her belly and noticed the blood in the water, and she swirled the water with her hand in a desperate attempt to hide it. She glanced around the room, checking faces to see if anyone had noticed. Behind one man's shoulder, the face of a statue stared back at her. *Artemis!* Her heart sank. She grabbed Nikias and held him, confident that his movement would keep the water swirling and hide the blood. "I'm taking him to the *frigidarium*," she told Philetus after touching his shoulder.

He turned from his conversation with the men near him and nodded in response. "I'll be there in a bit," he added. "We're discussing the healings that happened today." With that, Anthia escaped, taking Nikias with her.

．　■　．

In the warm room Anthia stirred the turnips and onions that were cooking in salt and olive oil on the brazier. Her aunt Eirene had already prepared the barley flour and oil, and she and Penelope were now forming the *maza* cakes. The children were playing, and Andrew would hopefully return soon from whatever work he had found that day in the agora. She was grateful to be able to sit while she worked, as it helped to keep the rag in place. She could hear Eutaxia and Lampo next door. For once they weren't arguing. *They actually sound like they're enjoying each other*, she marveled. They didn't ever argue in public, of course; Eutaxia was careful to be appropriately respectful and publicly honor her husband. In their one-room home, however, Eutaxia's strong opinions often made themselves known, as did Lampo's anger. But right now they were laughing quietly.

Someone knocked on their door, and Anthia could hear Lampo walk to answer it. "Father! Come in."

Anthia knew their arrival meant that Philetus had returned as well. Lampo had asked his cousin to find his parents, who lived on the other end of the city. They were Lampo's only immediate family in Ephesus, though of course there were cousins and other extended relatives. His father, Linus, had come to Ephesus to seek better prospects from Hypaipa, a village nearby, as a young man, bringing his new wife with him. His wife had given birth to Lampo first, but the three children born after him had not survived infancy. Lampo's mother had died in childbirth with the fifth baby, and the woman now married to his father was his stepmother, though she was nearer to Lampo's age than her husband's. Lampo's father, however, was still remarkably strong and healthy. His much younger wife had proven to be barren, so Lampo was his father's only hope for continuing the family line.

Anthia listened for her husband's voice but heard nothing. She turned to check on Nikias, who was supposed to be playing on the bedmat, but her eyes stopped when they reached the open doorway. Philetus stood there, a deep frown creasing his face. *What have I done now?* she wondered, sensing that the anger was directed at her.

"Why aren't you helping my cousin and Eutaxia right now?" Philetus demanded, striding toward her.

Anthia leaned back instinctively. "I am helping. I'm cooking food for tonight." She gestured toward the turnips and onions in the brazier. She dared not look at her aunt or Penelope, who continued their work on the *maza* cakes without commenting.

"You are too slow. This should be finished, and you should be next door, greeting Lampo's parents." Philetus insisted. "Get up now."

As she struggled to stand quickly, his hand reached for her arm. "Ouch!" she said, instantly wishing she could take the word back.

"Ouch?" he hissed quietly, aware of the thinness of the walls. "Ouch?" He stared at her and tightened his grip, watching her reaction. As the pain increased, Anthia forced herself to breathe normally.

"I am so sorry," she said quickly. "You are right. I am slow." Satisfied, he released her arm and turned toward Nikias, telling him to bring his toy and walk next door. "I'll be there in a moment," she promised.

■　■　■

The mood was celebratory, and Anthia did her best to pretend to join in. Her arm ached, but the growing pain in her abdomen concerned her the most. It didn't feel like contractions; Anthia was well aware of the distinct contours of that kind of pain. Phoebe's arrival had been a godsend. Phoebe took one look at her face and demanded that she sit and rest because of the advanced stage of her pregnancy. Philetus, unsure of how to respond, said nothing, which allowed Anthia some respite.

The whole group was packed into the one-room apartment shared by Lampo and Eutaxia, and the rest of the adults were still standing. Anthia, because of her position on the floor, was at eye level with the children, who were running and weaving through the adults. The conversation was focused on Euxinus and his amazing recovery, and Anthia was listening carefully. Lampo's father, while happy that his only grandchild was still alive, was concerned about the rising popularity of a new god in Ephesus. "At what point does this god's prominence begin to shame Artemis?" he asked worriedly. "There is also the question of Asclepius. . . . We live on the other side of the city, and we have heard as well about the other healings, including the casting out of evil spirits. If Artemis is shamed, that will only damage us as well."

"Please, sit and eat," Eutaxia invited, gesturing toward the plates and bowls of food that were placed in a circle in the middle of the room. They all sat, each with their legs crossed. An image flitted across Anthia's mind of all of them reclining, as the wealthy did, and she suppressed a smile. *We wouldn't all fit in this space if we were reclining.*

Philetus grabbed a sausage and wrapped it in a piece of flat cake. "I agree, Linus. We need to be careful. I wonder also about the man Paul, who teaches about Jesus and is healing in his name. Lampo," he added, turning to his cousin, "I've been thinking about what you said earlier—that he called you 'brother.' He's a Jew, so you obviously can't be related in any way. He's also a tentmaker—he works in a shop near our fishing stall in the agora—so he's an artisan, and based on what I've seen of the fine tents he makes and the elite customers he serves, he's of a higher status than we are. What do you make of that?"

Lampo hesitated, clearly searching for the right words. "I'm not sure."

Eutaxia spoke next. "I heard Paul teaching yesterday, and he said that Jesus changes the way that Jews interact with other people groups."

"How did you hear him teaching?" Lampo challenged.

"I needed thread to mend Euxinus's tunic, and I went to the agora while Phoebe and Anthia stayed with the children," she declared, defensive. She picked up a piece of *maza* and topped it with onion and turnip. "Anyway," she continued, "Paul said that Jesus is the first new human, and that all other humans can come together in unity and peace through him, or in him, or something. So maybe that's why Paul called you 'brother.' He thinks that because of Jesus you now share the same status."

Anthia wondered whether anyone was going to mention the other piece that was so confusing. *And Jesus died on a cross*, she added silently while she reached for an olive. But first Lampo's father had another question. Anthia had noticed that he was chewing very carefully, and he often raised his hand to his left cheek and held it there. *He must be in pain*, she realized. *Perhaps another one of his teeth is infected.* He only had a few teeth left anyway.

Anthia shuddered at the thought of the dentist and his dental tools near the agora, grateful again for her strong teeth. She still had most of them and hadn't had a toothache that resulted in a tooth being pulled since Nikias was little. She made a mental note to clean her teeth with her wool ball before bed that evening.

"Wait," Linus insisted. "This Jesus is the first new human? I thought he was a god. Didn't Paul say that he is healing only through the name and power of Jesus?"

"He is both, apparently," Zotike answered, and her husband nodded from his place next to her. "We're not sure if Jesus is like the emperor or if his 'man-ness' and 'god-ness' work differently," she added.

TEETH

The ancient world was not kind to teeth. Teeth were worn down from eating coarse grains. Abscesses and periodontal disease were rampant, and the solution for toothaches was often extraction. Tools for dentistry included extractors, scrapers, bone levers, scissors, small drills, and knives. Many elderly people, if they lived to old age, would have been toothless.

Physicians recommended cleaning teeth, often with a "toothbrush" composed of a wooden or bone stick with fibers and/or a sharp end to use as a pick. Fingers were also employed, either covered with cloth or small, round balls of wool that were dipped in honey, or a toothpaste or tooth powder (often used for whitening, not cleaning) made from shells, lime, chalk, dried whale's flesh and salt, or even animal ashes mixed with honey. Mouthwashes used vinegar and other ingredients such as pepper.

It appears that the causes of dental problems were not well understood, as small worms rather than plaque and bacteria were viewed as the reason. Medicines for toothache and/or rotting gums included ointments of oil; roots boiled in wine, vinegar, water, or salt; tree gum; smoke from burning seeds; and even eating mice or using the ash of burnt animal heads.

Anthia poured more wine into her cup. "Maybe he'll be teaching on that question tomorrow when we walk to our fish stall," she suggested.

"I've heard that he rises early to do his tentmaking work, and that at the midday break he always teaches and dialogues in the lecture hall, often staying all afternoon," Philetus added.

He's been paying closer attention than I thought! realized Anthia, and she wished that she could ask him what else he knew. *Or perhaps I can find a way to listen tomorrow. Perhaps...*

Day 4, Saturday

DAY OF SATURNUS/KRONOS

•◇•

ANTHIA PEERED INTO THE LECTURE HALL. It was empty, and busy pedestrians walked in front of it without so much as a second glance. *He must be working,* she considered. *Perhaps he's in the tentmaking shop.* She glanced again at the sun in the sky. *I have time,* she told herself. *It can't hurt just to walk by it.*

Philetus was fishing again, and she was assisting Eutaxia. Her friend was still being cautious in protecting her son, though Euxinus was doing very well. Eutaxia had kept him home this morning as she worked on her mending. Even one day of missed work had created quite a pile, and she needed to do her best to catch up. Her mending was part of the small fullery business where Lampo worked. He and a few other men purchased wool from weavers, including the family operation that Phoebe and her husband were part of, and finished it, making it into usable fabric for clothing. They also cleaned clothing, a messy and time-consuming process.

Anthia readjusted her grip on Nikias's hand and strode toward the agora. *Vegetables, garum, flour,* she repeated to herself. The sun was shining but the day was still pleasantly warm—not yet hot—and Anthia decided to browse a bit. She also wanted to distract herself from the continued bleeding and reduced movement of the baby. *I'm just looking for the best deals for Eutaxia*, she told herself as she pushed on her belly again, hoping for a response. *I need to see what my options are.* She entered the agora through her typical gate on the southern side. She normally turned right, so this time she took a left and noticed a vendor selling garum. The woman caught her eye and began to call out to her to come. Anthia noted the size of the bottles—*too small!*—and smiled and walked past, determined to find a better option.

As she walked she scanned both the shops around the edges and the temporary stalls, often set up in tents, that vendors and merchants used to sell or trade their goods in the interior of the agora. She walked past a statue of the emperor that had been erected when she was younger. *Hail, Claudius*, she mimicked silently. *I've certainly heard that enough times from all the politicians and Roman citizens around here.* She paused for a few moments near a food vendor, watching the woman make sausages while she breathed in the aroma of the cooking meat. The woman was scooping a mixture of animal organs and spices into pig intestines that she was using as casings. *She doesn't have any teeth*, Anthia realized suddenly. As if hearing her thoughts, the woman looked up and smiled at her. *No teeth.* She smiled back. *That's a good job for her. At least she can eat what she doesn't sell, since sausages are so soft.* Anthia took one more deep breath, her mouth watering, and moved on.

A shop on her left was neatly organized with tables and shelves, on top of which were sets of weights. The woman working the counter was clearly supervising the young girl at her side, who was scooping flour into a clay pot to be weighed. "Is this right, Mama?" the young girl asked hesitantly.

"Yes," the woman confirmed, adjusting the scale while a customer watched. Behind them a young man was directing a blindfolded donkey; the animal was walking in a tight circle, grinding the wheat between two large stones into fine flour. *Finely ground flour—what a treat!* Anthia thought, then modified her internal monologue as she noticed the customer's attire. The woman was wearing a *stola*, the traditional dress of a female Roman citizen. *Not a treat for her. This is daily life.*

Nikias pulled away from her hand, and she let him run. He quickly joined a group of other toddlers who were playing with a pile of small sticks in front of a vegetable stall. Anthia approached, offering a smile to the women behind the makeshift counter. She surveyed the turnips and garlic, trying to decide. Suddenly a man walked up from the direction of the western gate and set down a basket of onions. He quickly turned and headed back to his cart, and Anthia knew that her decision had been made. "How much for two onions and two turnips?" she asked, prepared to haggle.

The woman's reply was instant. "Five quadrantes."

Four quadrantes equaled one as, and sixteen asses equaled one denarius, a typical day's wage for a day laborer. She shook her head quickly. "Two."

The woman surveyed Anthia more closely, her eyes narrowing. "Four."

"I have family who grow turnips," she lied, "and I know that turnips have been growing well. Two quadrantes."

The woman exhaled. "Three."

"Done." Anthia smiled, proud of herself; her haggling skills were impressive. *I think people underestimate me. I don't look like I'd be good at this, but I am.* The searing heat from a corner blacksmith shop caused her to take a few steps toward the interior of the agora. She glanced inside, noting that a pair of blacksmiths were working together. *One is a woman!* she realized, silently congratulating the woman's physical strength and wondering about the woman's husband, whom she assumed was the other blacksmith. *I haven't seen that before. That's new.* In Ephesus, however, there was always something new.

Garum, flour, garum, flour, she reminded herself, though she couldn't help but pause in front of a dye shop. She smelled it first, thinking not for the first time that dyers smelled just as pungent as fishmongers, though the smells were different. She could see the vats of soaking wool near the front, while behind them the lead cauldrons of dye were being heated over firepots. She watched a young woman stir a cauldron with a pole, noting that her hair was matted with sweat around her face. *You'll be even hotter when you're pregnant,* she warned silently, though the woman's red tunic was an impressive advertisement for their work in the shop. She glanced down at her own gray tunic and moved on.

Next door was a tavern, and the smell of beer, warm bread, and cooked meat wafted out. A young waitress was carrying a tray filled with ceramic mugs, and she stopped at a low table surrounded by

---

DYEING

Access to dyed items, including clothing, was only possible for the wealthier population in the ancient world, who used it as one way to signal their social status and class. Purple was especially popular among Roman senators and other wealthy citizens. Those lower on the status ladder wore creams, grays, browns, and blacks, the natural colors of wool. Dyeing required extensive plant and animal materials, as well as chemicals such as iron salts or alum. Reds were often made from plants or insect larvae, blues from berries such as whortleberry, and purple from mollusks. Often a pound of dye was required for a pound of wool. Dyers often specialized in particular colors.

men on benches. As she placed their drinks on the table, one of the men's hands grasped her thigh and crept upward underneath her tunic. She stood as if frozen while the other men laughed, her face turning even paler than the white powder that she wore. The man who was touching her nodded to another man seated behind a counter. *Her owner*, Anthia realized. The serving girl was a slave, and her body was available as well. The man behind the counter stood and walked over to the group. It was clear that the girl's behavior wasn't pleasing to him, but a swift slap on the back of her head helped to change her demeanor. She smiled and leaned into the customer's chest, whispering something to him that only made him laugh harder. He grabbed her by the wrist and half-dragged her to the stairs at the back of the tavern. As he pulled her up the stairs, another man squeezed past them on his way down.

Philetus. Anthia glanced quickly around, checking to see whether any of their family or friends were watching Philetus's departure. She breathed a sigh of relief that it seemed he hadn't been spotted—but then she wondered at the cost of such a visit. *Where did he find the money? Or did he make a trade?* Anthia kept walking, grateful that Nikias had not spotted his father and that Philetus had not noticed her.

A pack of wild dogs ran across her path, and Anthia jumped back, anxiously searching for Nikias. *There he is.* Several young men armed with sticks and rocks chased the dogs; she had seen similar mobs kill dogs before. Somewhat ironically, there was a man in a toga in front of her who was carrying a small dog that was now yipping furiously in the direction where the other dogs had run.

Someone called her name, and she turned to see Sulpicia, a woman who, along with her husband, worked as a fuller in the same shop as Lampo. Anthia approached the counter at their shop and greeted her friend, and at the sound of her voice

COSMETICS

The use of cosmetics was fairly common in the ancient world, though because of the cost they were more associated with the wealthy and/or prostitutes. Eyebrows were darkened with black and brown liners (often made from kohl); cheek rouge was created from wine, red ochre, and plants; and pale complexions were accentuated and embellished with powders and creams made from white chalk, lead, or marl. Shells were often used as containers.

Lampo stopped jumping on the terra cotta pressing bowl that was being used to soak and clean the clothes inside it. His face registered concern as he used the hand rest he had been clasping to adjust his body to face Anthia's direction. "Is it Euxinus? Is he all right?"

"Oh, yes, he's fine. I'm just getting a few things for Eutaxia, since she's trying to catch up on the mending."

Lampo nodded and went back to his work, jumping again and again on the pressing bowl. "Please tell Eutaxia that I will not be back at midday; I need to catch up from yesterday and collect the urine jars from around the city."

Anthia said that she would, and Sulpicia then leaned forward to whisper conspiratorially. "We need to talk. I want to hear all about it, both Euxinus and the man with the evil spirit yesterday. I heard you were there." Another customer walked up to the counter, and Anthia backed away, telling Sulpicia that she would see her later.

The smell of baking bread greeted her as she turned right once again and approached the north gate. Several loaves of fresh bread were being placed on the wooden counter, and Anthia

LAUNDRY AND FULLERS

Fulleries were the laundromats of the ancient world, but fullers also prepared new textiles. In washing, fullers used natural clays such as fuller's earth to absorb grease and other dirt. Raw material such as wool often contained burrs, dirt, and the animal's fat, lanolin, or grease. Potash and soapwort were other common cleaning agents, as was human urine, which (often when fermented) was well known as a detergent, especially in cleaning white material. Fullers often dispersed urine jars around their city, which were collected when full. In Ostia a local public latrine was even connected to a neighboring fullery by means of a lead pipe that could deliver the urine.

Washing, soaking, and shrinking were accomplished with large basins covered with pressing bowls on which fullers jumped or danced occasionally. This process could take days, especially as cloth was normally washed twice, with a beating in between. After drying it was brushed or carded with plants such as thistles or even hedgehog skin. Shearing was also sometimes needed in order to smooth the surface. (Discarded lint or nap was not wasted but used to stuff items such as pillows.) Bleaching often came next and was executed by burning sulfur under exposed material. Such an extensive process was obviously expensive, thus limiting its regular access to the wealthy.

Fulleries ranged in size from small (perhaps five employees) to large (as many as twenty employees). Fullers often organized themselves into local guilds for their mutual benefit as well as for the honoring of their patron goddess, Minerva. Being a fuller was foul-smelling and dangerous work; exposure to various chemicals and sulfur affected the skin and lungs.

gazed enviously at them as wealthier customers got in line to buy them. *At least we have food to eat today and a brazier to bake bread*, she affirmed, willing herself to believe it. She craned her neck to see over the heads of the people waiting, appreciating the ovens lining the back of the shop.

Across from the bakery was a grain stall, and Anthia walked over to survey the selection. *Wheat, barley, millet, emmer, rye.* She fingered the small coins in her pocket, estimating how much she could purchase. She asked for a price on the wheat and haggled the vendor down a bit. Placing the wheat in her small cloth bag, she walked ahead to where she knew a milling shop was located. Again she negotiated, finally settling on an acceptable amount. She watched as a young man funneled her wheat into the hole on the top milling stone. Several rotations later, he stopped the donkey and scooped the roughly ground flour into a ceramic pot. He handed it to the woman working the counter, who kept the amount they had agreed on and gave the rest to Anthia. *That should be enough for a whole loaf of bread for tonight*, she thought. She wished that she could do her own shopping as well, but until Philetus returned with fish to sell, she had no coins or fish to use in trade. Again she wondered how he had paid for his visit to the brothel.

Conveniently, a garum stall had been set up under a tent next to the miller, and Anthia was pleased when she saw the larger bottles of garum. As she surveyed the selection she felt a tap on her shoulder. Turning, her eyes met those of Iarine, a distant cousin of Phoebe's. The women had both been present at the birth of Phoebe's youngest child, and Iarine pointed to Anthia's belly with a smile. "Your baby is coming soon."

"Yes, soon." Anthia gave Iarine a quick hug. "It's good to see you."

Iarine held up a pile of clothing. "This needs tailoring, and soon, but stop by the shop when you can."

"I will," Anthia replied, nodding, then turned back toward the garum selection. "Where was this made?" she questioned the child who was seated behind the selection. The boy, who looked to be about five or six years old, turned to a woman in the back of the tent who was nursing an infant. "Pompeii," she said. Impressed, Anthia asked for a price.

The amount the child mentioned was so high that Anthia gasped audibly. "Thank you," she said softly, walking away. *It's just fermented fish sauce*, she told herself, though she knew that the Italian factories were said to make the finest batches of the sweet-and-sour sauce in their big, open tanks. *That garum stall is only for the politicians and rich Roman citizens.*

In the usually empty space on the other side of the north gate a slaver had set up shop. *A slave boat must have come into the harbor this morning*, she realized, surveying the merchandise. Anthia's family had never owned slaves; people from their status level usually didn't. Her eyes fell on a woman about her age who was nursing an infant, and involuntarily Anthia glanced back toward the garum stall with the other nursing mother. Like the other slaves, this young woman was almost naked, wearing just a cloth wrapped around her thighs and hips. Her large breasts hung free, and the one that was not being used to nurse the baby was leaking a steady stream of milk. As she watched, a tall man with coarse black hair and skin almost the same color walked up to the woman and inspected her carefully, surveying each part of her body as he lifted her arms and walked around her.

"How much," he asked the slaver, "just for the woman?"

"You don't want the child as well? He looks strong and healthy, and in a few years he will be able to work hard."

"No," the customer deferred. "I need the woman as a wet nurse, and I don't want the milk being shared with my sons. They are twins."

They haggled over the price, starting at 280 denarii, as she watched. The price, while almost a year's wages for some, was for others a small amount to pay. Anthia glanced down the row at the others, noting the varied ages, skin colors, and builds. She watched as a female customer inspected a young girl, and a man in the toga of a Roman citizen walked around a large male slave with the palest skin Anthia had ever seen.

Anthia's eyes skipped to the next shop, where pigs were being sold. Both adult pigs and piglets were on offer, and part of the space was partitioned as a butcher shop. Slabs of pork hung on

---

SLAVERY

Slavery was commonplace in the Roman Empire, with estimates as high as 20 to 30 percent of the population at various times. Slaves could be purchased in marketplaces in every major city. One became a slave through a variety of means, including being born to a slave, being taken during conquest or by pirates, selling oneself to repay debt or because the family was in dire financial straits, and exposure of unwanted infants. There is no evidence for slavery being related to modern conceptions of race.

Slaves were the lowest class of people, though slaves owned by the elite benefited from the higher status of their owners. Some such slaves were educated or were able to acquire their own slaves and amass wealth. Slaves were also at times manumitted, or freed, because of the gratitude of an owner or the ability to pay for their own freedom.

Slaves were the legal property of their owners and could be used in whatever way their owners wished, including sexual pleasure. Abuse was common, and runaway slaves hoping to escape abuse were often punished severely or even killed by crucifixion if caught.

hooks and rested on the counter. Anthia noticed the sausage vendor from earlier waiting in line; apparently she already needed more offal.

She crossed in front of the area where this afternoon, hopefully, their fish stall would be set up. "Please, Glaukos, send fish to their nets," she offered quietly. Nikias looked up at her when she spoke, his eyes curious. "Pray to the fish god with me, Nikias. May he bless us today with a large catch."

"Fish!" screamed Nikias, darting away once again. She let out a low chuckle, walking to her usual garum stall. The merchant who owned it purchased large quantities of garum from factories in the province, and his prices were always fair. She bought a nice bottle with minimal haggling and walked toward Iarine's tailor shop, looking for her friend's face.

Where is she? Iarine was almost always at the shop, working with a group of both men and women. Suddenly Anthia felt the gush of blood, and she halted her pace. She looked for a place to sit, needing to control the bleeding. Up ahead she saw the tent-making shop, and a crowd of women gathered inside it. *Perhaps there*, she decided, noticing Iarine's profile among the women. Her fiery red hair was difficult to miss. She took Nikias's hand, pulling him away from the wall where he was scratching lines with a small rock, and walked past a poultry vendor on the way to her destination.

Iarine and the other women stood in a circle around another woman whose face Anthia couldn't see. She squeezed her way into the shop and then sat down quickly with Nikias in her lap. She wished she could see, but at least this way she could attempt to manage the bleeding. The woman in the middle was speaking.

"Yes, it is Jesus who has the ultimate power to heal. Before his death and resurrection he healed many people in the province of Judea, where he lived. Healings are one of the signs that the kingdom of the one true god is being powerfully established, for this kingdom is one of healing and restoration."

A woman who stood directly in front of Anthia responded, and Anthia stared at her back as she spoke, admiring the fine leather of her sandals. "But Priscilla, how does this power and name of Jesus work? I heard that Paul gave some people an article of clothing that then healed the sick or exorcised demons, but a friend told me this morning that she knows someone who was healed by an apron that Paul didn't give him. Paul touched it, but Paul didn't give it to him. What do you make of that?"

Priscilla answered calmly. "The power of Jesus is big, so much bigger than human attempts to confine it or limit how it is used. He stands above all other powers."

All powers, pondered Anthia silently. *Even Artemis? Could the power of Jesus really save me and my baby?*

The woman in front of her spoke again, and it was as if she were reading Anthia's mind. "Even Artemis? Even Asclepius?"

"Yes," Priscilla insisted, "for those are our true adversaries. They are the powers that control the darkness and its armies."

The woman's response was sarcastic this time, and Anthia watched as the woman's body language mirrored her tone. She arched her back and tilted her head, the braids of her golden hair moving softly as she did so. "Adversaries? Please, Priscilla . . ." and then she paused, clearly searching for the right words.

Anthia smiled. *She reminds me of Eutaxia.*

Priscilla took advantage of the silence, adding quickly, "Friends, I don't want us to lose sight of the bigger picture. Jesus is the true savior, the true lord, and these healings and exorcisms are a demonstration of that. He calls us to respond and commit to his lordship with our lives."

Priscilla's dialogue partner had an immediate response to that comment. "So he's the true savior and lord, but he lets us decide whether to give him our allegiance? I've never heard of such a thing. When the emperor or Artemis claims supremacy, we just defer to the reality."

Anthia nodded vigorously, silently thanking the woman for asking such a relevant question. Priscilla's response was again given calmly. "Yes. That's one of the ways—the many, many ways—that Jesus is different from our emperors and goddesses like Artemis."

The conversation continued as other women joined in, and Anthia listened quietly while she examined a curved needle and waxed thread that sat on a low table near her. Also on the table was a piece of cloth that appeared to be made from some kind of animal hair. It had holes punched into it. *It doesn't look big enough to be a tent*, she reflected. *Perhaps a sun shade?*

Suddenly a woman from the other side of the circle exclaimed loudly that she needed to leave because her husband was waiting for her at their perfume stall. Instantly an image of a tiny curly-haired woman appeared in Anthia's mind, and Anthia wondered whether it was indeed the woman she walked past every day. Other women followed, and the group dispersed.

As the group thinned, Anthia glanced around furtively. Her eyes met Iarine's bright green ones, and her friend's arched eyebrows asked the question for her. "I'm bleeding," Anthia confessed. "I had to sit down."

Concerned, Iarine knelt beside her. "How long have you been bleeding?"

"Several days."

"Priscilla," Iarine called out, "do you have any rags?"

Priscilla approached and smiled warmly, and Anthia couldn't help but notice the evenness of her teeth. "Yes, yes, of course. Is this your friend?"

"We grew up near each other. She sells the fish that her husband catches in a stall nearby." Iarine paused. "She is bleeding."

Priscilla motioned to a small room attached to the back of the shop. "Would you like to lie down? There is plenty of room." Anthia nodded gratefully, and the women helped her stand so that she could walk to the bedmat. Priscilla left, then returned with two small rags and a cup of water. "I'll be out front," she stated.

Anthia took the opportunity and plunged in with rapid-fire questions, hoping to find answers from her friend. "How do you know Priscilla? And do you know Paul? And what do you know about Jesus? Eutaxia's son Euxinus was healed through a hand-kerchief yesterday that Paul gave her husband. I also saw a demon—or some demons, I'm not really sure—leave a man yes-terday because of another cloth that Paul had touched. Have you heard about that?" She stopped suddenly, feeling foolish, but Iarine just smiled and touched her arm.

Iarine smiled, a thoughtful look on her face. "Yes, I've heard about all of it, and I know Paul." She paused. "We have joined the Way," she said, looking at Anthia directly. "We are now part of the group of people throughout the world who prepare for and participate in the true god's rule. Our allegiance is with Jesus, who is this god in human form. Jesus comforts, heals, restores, and makes it possible for people of different tribes and peoples to come together as brothers and sisters." She paused again, then added, "He also judges, as the true sovereign should."

Anthia digested this information, filtering what she knew of Hero, Iarine's husband, with the idea of him joining a community of people whose leader was a crucified Jew. "How did you decide to do this? What compelled you?" she asked. "And how do you know Priscilla?"

Iarine settled in, sitting cross-legged on the floor next to the mat. "It's a surprising story, and when I think about it I'm still a little overwhelmed myself. It started a while ago when I met Priscilla. She had just come to Ephesus. I met her at the fountain one morning when we were getting water for the day. She was helping an elderly woman get a drink, and my mother always used to do that. We started talking, and I kept seeing her every morning. She eventually told me why they were here."

"Why are they here?" Anthia whispered, though she almost feared that she knew the answer.

"To declare to Ephesus and the whole province of Asia that the true lord of the world is Jesus." Iarine chuckled softly, shaking her head. "It caught me off-guard the first time too. I wanted to dismiss the idea, but I couldn't. I liked Priscilla so much—respected her—and by that time I'd started visiting her here in the shop." She gestured around the room with her hand. "They live here, the three of them, behind the shop. For a while it was just Priscilla and her husband, but then Paul joined them. I'd been watching Priscilla and her husband interact day after day, and I would ask Priscilla questions about Jesus once in a while."

Anthia hesitated, then asked, "Why would anyone think that a crucified Jew could be lord of the world?"

"That was one of my many questions, and let me tell you, the answer to that is big. But it has to do with how this god operates and what he prioritizes. Priscilla is always saying that Jesus turns everything upside down in terms of power and status. 'Strength through weakness' is her favorite phrase, I think."

"Well, I'm certainly weak, and no one would say that I'm important," Anthia reflected. "I'm not sure how that could equal strength. So . . . how did Hero become convinced?"

"Aquila, Priscilla's husband, needed a tailor. He came to our shop, and Hero did the work for him. They became friends, often going to the taverns and baths together. Then he met a Jewish man named Apollos, and that was it. He was such an amazing speaker, so convincing. He spent a lot of time with other Jews in the synagogue across town—I think that's where they met him—but Priscilla and

Aquila hosted him here quite often. They would all eat dinner together, talking about Jesus long into the night, and they often invited Hero and me to join them." She looked around the small room with satisfaction. "We spent many amazing evenings here."

"I didn't realize that you two had so many Jewish friends." Anthia's question was half-jest, half-serious.

"Hero grew up next to a Jewish family. He played with their sons and daughters often when he was young. The Jews don't practice infanticide or infant exposure, so there were a lot of kids running around. He was always impressed by their commitment to their god and the way they treated each other, especially the youngest daughter, who has a leg deformity and can't walk." She shrugged.

"So this was your husband's decision, and you went along with it?"

Iarine shook her head. "I agreed with him, but my reasons may be a bit different. I love what I've seen of Priscilla's marriage. Priscilla herself is just amazing as well, and the way that Aquila treats her and talks about her is inspiring."

"How so?"

"Well, he clearly respects his wife and loves her deeply. I've seen that in other marriages, but I don't think I've ever seen a husband act so self-sacrificially toward his wife. He puts her first all the time. I've never seen him hit or push her, or even speak disrespectfully to her. I asked Priscilla about it, and she said that he's the same way in private. He also doesn't visit the brothels."

This last statement really caught Anthia's attention. "He only has sex with her? Why?"

"Hero told me that the Jews believe that spouses should not have other sexual partners, and Priscilla said that marriage is like the relationship Jesus has with his followers. He is loyal to them, and they are loyal to him. He sacrificed his life for them, so they should sacrifice their lives for him." She lifted the cup, handing it to Anthia. "Drink."

"When Paul came back to Ephesus," Iarine continued, "he was so grateful for them, to them. Both of them. I've heard him call both Aquila and Priscilla his fellow workers in Jesus. He approved of the way that both Priscilla and Aquila taught Apollos. I've heard of women teachers or philosophers, but I've never seen or known one. Until now."

"Is this Apollos still here?"

"No, he left before Paul came back."

"I've seen and heard Paul in the lecture hall of Tyrannus. Philetus and I stood outside with the crowds to listen to the dialogue."

Iarine nodded. "When Paul first came back he spent time in the synagogue, not the lecture hall. That lasted until some Jews who disagreed with him about Jesus started slandering him and the Way. Then he went to the lecture hall, and some of the Jews who were convinced about Jesus went with him. One of them, Dorcas, pays for the hall."

"They slandered him? How did Paul respond to this attack on his honor? Did he return it?"

"No, he refused to slander them! He could have, but he didn't. We asked him why, and he said that Jesus didn't respond in kind when he was slandered. His mantra is, 'When reviled, we bless; when persecuted, we endure; when slandered, we speak kindly.' I'm still trying to make sense of it." Iarine paused, then added, "You're welcome to join us tomorrow when we gather as the Way. We meet right here after the workday ends. People bring food to share for dinner, but you could just come. You and Philetus. And bring Nikias; there are tons of kids running around."

"I'll try to talk with Philetus," she said, wondering how she could bring up a controversial idea like that without putting her husband in a bad mood and possibly endangering herself.

Iarine stood. "I have to go back to my shop—I need to begin tailoring those *stola*s and tunics I was carrying earlier—but I'll be back as soon as I can to check on you."

As soon as she left Priscilla popped her head into the back room. "Please excuse my poor hospitality, but I have a customer who is coming later today to pick up his tent, and it's not quite finished. If you hear men's voices it's probably just Paul and Aquila returning; they went to the harbor to pick up some goat hair that we ordered from a merchant whose ship docked this morning." She smiled briefly. "Paul's convinced it's the best material for making tents, but I think he's just biased because they're his hometown goats."

Paul! The name hit Anthia like a thunderbolt. She couldn't help but hope that he would come soon. *Maybe he'll talk more about Jesus. Maybe, with Priscilla and her husband as part of the conversation, I can eavesdrop and get some answers.* While she used the rags Priscilla had given her, Nikias ran in circles, flailing his arms in all directions. She could hear the carpenters in the shop next door, pounding away. She had seen the benches, tables, and chairs displayed often in the front of their shop, as well as the wealthy people who could afford to buy them browsing and bargaining. She suddenly felt exhausted, and she looked at Nikias, who was now lying on the floor and playing with a couple of rocks. She pulled him toward her, and when he settled in, her eyes began to close. *Just for a moment*, she told herself.

■　■　■

"Priscilla!" a male voice called out suddenly, waking Anthia from her nap. "We have food!"

Priscilla laughed heartily. "But the better question is, do you have the goat hair?"

"We do," the male voice insisted.

The now-familiar voice of Paul joined in. "We stopped at a vendor for salted fava beans with oil. We know they're your favorite."

Anthia's mouth watered. Fava beans were one of her favorites as well, and it had been a long time since she had been able to purchase the prepared treat from a market vendor. The smell of the sautéed beans wafted back to the room, and she closed her eyes and inhaled.

"I'm glad that you brought so much," Priscilla announced. "We have guests in the back room who are likely hungry. A friend of Iarine's and her young son are resting on the bedmat."

Just then Iarine returned, greeting the men and Priscilla warmly. "There's enough for you as well, sister," Paul encouraged.

Sister?! Is Iarine somehow related to Paul? Anthia's thoughts raced as she considered the possibilities. She was still thinking about it when Iarine ducked through the low doorway with a handful of beans.

"Here," she insisted. "For you and Nikias."

"Thank you." She paused, then blurted out, "Are you related to Paul?"

Looking surprised by the question, Iarine answered. "No, we do not share blood. But we are brothers and sisters in Jesus."

Anthia shivered involuntarily. "And that's why they're sharing food with you?"

Anthia watched as Iarine popped a couple of beans into her mouth. "Yes," she said simply. "We are kin, and we share resources as kin do."

Anthia ate silently for a few moments, chewing while she placed another couple of beans in Nikias's outstretched hand. "I must get going," she said after a few moments. "Eutaxia will be waiting for me." She stood up in the awkward manner that she had come to think of as her pregnancy reality, first half rolling onto her side, which allowed her to push herself up with her hands.

"You're always welcome," Iarine added, scooping up Nikias for a hug as they walked to the front room.

Both Paul and Aquila were busy dealing with another customer, but the women were able to talk to Priscilla, who was busy sewing. All that Anthia could manage in the moment was a brief "thank you," but Priscilla still smiled warmly.

"You're welcome. And please, join us tomorrow night at sundown if you can. We'd love to have you." She went back to work, and Anthia raced from the shop, her heart pounding. She turned to look back only once and found Paul's eyes looking at her curiously. She lifted Nikias and ran.

Why am I running? she asked herself after just a few steps. *I can't run with Nikias. I can't even run by myself right now, not with this belly.* She forced herself to slow down and walk, pacing herself and breathing as deeply as possible. *I'm fine*, she told herself as she walked in front of a stall displaying rabbits and other wild game for sale. *I feel much better.* And she did, she realized. *Except I need to use the latrine.* She considered the possibility of waiting until she reached the public toilets nearer her *insula* but decided that it would be painful to try and wait that long. *I'll use the one outside the south gate, the gate of Mazeus and Mithridates. Then I'll rush back to Eutaxia, who's probably wondering where I've been.*

She realized after a moment that she was matching her pace to the sound of music, and she turned toward the center of the agora to see who was playing. The two flutists and cymbalist were younger than her—*maybe fifteen or sixteen?*—she thought idly, and they were dressed in material that was almost translucent. They swayed with the music, moving around a young man in a mask who was performing a pantomime routine. The sexual act being imitated was clear, and the crowd responded with approval; several men shouted out invitations to the performers. A well-dressed man then stepped forward and announced their performance tonight in the theater, inviting all to pay the fee and be entertained. A second well-dressed man—this one in a white toga with a purple stripe, a clear sign of his Roman citizenship and high status—stepped forward and loudly announced that he would be honored to pay the fee for all attendees that evening. *And he'll probably have his generosity as a patron engraved on a plaque for all to see in the agora.... Part of me wants to attend,* she admitted to herself. She could picture the many beautiful statues of Cupids and Nike that adorned the stage, another gift from a generous donor.

Figure 4.1. The ancient Ephesian theater

The last shop she passed on her way out of the gate was a perfumery, and the combination of smells brought a wave of nausea. *Always,* she mourned. *I am so sensitive to smells when I'm pregnant. It's like my nose decides that it should compete with the noses of dogs. Ugh.* She walked past as quickly as possible and exited the agora. She stopped at the latrine, grateful for the semi-darkness as she surveyed once again the blood on her thighs. She rinsed Nikias's fingers in the basin along with her own, then adjusted the bag of food and took his hand for the walk home.

PERFUMERY

Perfumes were yet another luxury item afforded only by the wealthy, and even those who produced and traded them often ran in elite circles. Producing perfume was expensive and time consuming, a cultivated skill that, along with recipes for perfumes, was passed down in families.

Perfumes could be dry or take the form of a paste or liquid, and they were made with a variety of ingredients and methods, from soaking flower petals and leaves in liquids (such as grape juice or olive oil) to combining the fat and marrow of bulls and calves with wine and spices such as cinnamon, cardamom, and nard. Myrrh, frankincense, saffron, aloe, resin, almonds, honey, lavender, and fennel were other common ingredients. The mixtures were often heated, after which they would be strained. Perfumes were often stored and sold in cloth or small flasks, vases, or boxes and were used both for secular and religious purposes, such as enhancing sexual appeal (including for pros-

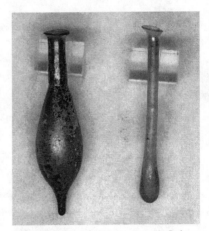

Figure 4.2. Perfume and/or makeup vessels. Perfumes were affordable only for the wealthy

titutes), advertising status, for bathing and funeral rituals, and in social settings such as dinner parties (where guests' feet were sometimes washed with perfumed water) and performances in theaters (where the audience might be sprinkled with a perfumed water mixture).

She began the climb up to their top-floor home. At Eutaxia's door she knocked quickly but entered without waiting for a response. Eutaxia was sitting with her mending, as Anthia expected, but Euxinus was not sitting with her. Anthia laughed out loud as she watched him do a somersault. "Wow, he's definitely feeling better." Nikias rushed to join his playmate, and Anthia carried the market items over to her friend.

"Before I forget, Lampo said that he won't be coming back until this evening. He needs to work through the rest period because he's behind."

"Like me." Eutaxia pointed to the pile, which was noticeably smaller than it had been that morning.

"Nice work, friend!" Anthia congratulated her. She set the garum and vegetables down before holding out the flour for Eutaxia to see. "Does this meet your approval?"

"Yes, and those vegetables are beautiful. Do you mind getting the bread started while you wait for Philetus?"

"Of course not!" Anthia sat quickly, and Eutaxia's keen eyes noticed.

"You're bleeding again." It was a statement, not a question.

"Yes," Anthia admitted. "And I haven't felt the baby kick all morning."

Eutaxia pursed her lips, thinking. "Okay, here's what we'll do. You can help with the dough, but then you need to go home and rest. I'll keep Nikias for a bit so that you can sleep, hopefully." She pulled last night's leftovers from a small shelf. "Here, eat a few bites of bread—and some olives—first."

Anthia accepted the food, then added in as innocent a tone as she could muster, "Thank you, I will. I did already have some fava beans, however." She paused for effect. "At the tentmaking shop of Paul."

She may as well have shouted the news at Eutaxia, because the effect was the same. Eutaxia's face quickly moved from an expression of astonishment to curiosity. "How did that happen? Tell me everything." As they ate and worked, feeding the children bites of food between somersaults, Anthia shared the whole story.

"The question now," Eutaxia stated, "is whether you're going to visit the gathering or not."

They were interrupted by the arrival of Philetus, who opened the door loudly and then stood swaying in the doorway. The women exchanged knowing glances before Eutaxia repeated her earlier decision. "Go with Philetus and rest. I'll keep Nikias for a while."

In their home next door Philetus leaned into Anthia, kissing her sloppily as he wrapped his arms around her. *Drunk*, she confirmed as she tasted the beer on his tongue. She also caught the faint scent of perfume, and the memory of him on the brothel stairs returned. She wanted to ask him pointedly what money or fish he'd used, as well as why he was drunk when it was only midday, but she feared the repercussions of being impertinent. She had enough pain and bleeding without being hit by her drunken husband.

"Praise be to Glauuuuukos," Philetus slurred, then shook his head and spoke more carefully. "He honored us with a large catch this morning. As soon as we dropped our nets."

Ahh, that was it. He was celebrating, she thought silently. "Was Galleos with you today?" she asked, and Philetus nodded as he sat and then lay down on the bedmat.

"Yes. We caught the fish and sent most of them with his sons to a fish-salting shop. The owner of the shop placed the order with Galleos last night. We brought the rest alive to a Roman politician who wanted them for his fish tank. He plans to have his own little fish hatchery. He lives in one of the terraced homes just down the street from the agora's south entrance. He paid us well for them."

Anthia watched him, thinking he had fallen asleep. "Primigenia," he said softly, rolling from his back to his side.

So that's her name. Anthia was grateful that no one else was paying attention. She just hoped he hadn't spent too much on the girl; the price could vary widely, from the price of a glass of wine or meal all the way up to a typical full day's wage.

She didn't blame him for it. *That's just how men act,* she reflected, recalling her mother's advice to her when she became a woman. *In some ways it's actually a relief. With this belly I'm not in the mood to service my husband.* But then, unbidden, Iarine's words about her husband's refusal to visit the brothels came to mind. She shook her head to clear it and laid down next to her husband. *Time to rest,* she instructed herself.

Day 5, Sunday

DAY OF SOL/HELIOS

ANTHIA STOOD BEHIND THE COUNTER OF THEIR FISH STALL. *I wish I could sit*, she thought for the hundredth time. *My back hurts so much. And my feet.* She sighed, adjusting her position in an attempt to get comfortable. Adding to her burden was the fact that she hadn't felt the baby kick all day. *What can I do?* she asked herself again. Another customer approached, and she attempted a smile as the man stopped at the counter. His small black eyes surveyed the fish, eventually stopping on a mackerel.

"How much?" he asked, and they began their haggling. Anthia's heart wasn't in it, though she was grateful for the large catch of fish that Philetus and Galleos had once again caught this morning. She and the customer finally agreed on a price, and he reached into a fine leather pouch and extracted the necessary coins. He tucked the pouch back into the waistband of his beautifully dyed tunic—*bright blue!*—paid, and left with the fish. She eyed the sun, which was low in the sky. Her heart raced as she thought once again of Iarine's invitation. Part of her was curious, of course. She wondered about the people who had committed themselves to following a man who had been crucified by the Romans. Part of her was disdainful. *Crucified*, she thought again.

Crucified. Like a slave. Or a criminal. But the biggest part of her was afraid. She knew the risk of shame with participating in a new religious group, one that wasn't sanctioned by the city or the Romans. Beyond the legal risks were the even more important relational ones. *What might happen to our ties with our fishing association, or our families, or our friends, if they disapprove of this? What might this cost me, cost us?*

She knew she was getting ahead of herself. She hadn't even talked to Philetus about the possibility of visiting the gathering of the Way. She knew the chances of him being interested were slim; he cared deeply about the reputation especially of their fishing association, and he would likely be unwilling to risk any slight to its honor. She wondered again whether she could find an excuse to go alone or with Nikias. As she was pondering this possibility, her husband returned from the latrine, grinning from ear to ear. She smiled back, arching her eyebrows in question.

"We did it!" Philetus exclaimed, pounding Galleos, who stood beside him, on the back. "The owner of the fish salting shop, Phygelus, was so pleased with our catch yesterday that he wants to discuss the possibility of a regular contract." His eyes gleamed. "We are meeting him at a tavern on the other side of the city near his shop at sundown to discuss it." He glanced down at the two fish that had yet to be sold. Galleos stepped forward and gestured to his wife, Euippe, with his hand. "Be sure to sell the fish with Anthia," he commanded, "and then go home with Eubulus and Manilia." He paused. "Where are the twins?"

"Playing with Nikias," Euippe answered softly. Her eyes searched the nearby agora, and then she pointed with her left hand. "There they are."

Galleos nodded, then added, "I'm taking Crescens and Trophimus with me. They need to learn how to set up a contract." His wife nodded in response, and Anthia noted the presence of the teenage sons behind their father. They stood with their chests out, clearly proud to be included in this aspect of the family business. *As they should be.* She noted with some surprise that their jaws and upper lips now showed the shadows of hair growth. *They are near adulthood, soon to take wives.*

"Take Nikias home, and I'll be back later," Philetus said as he turned away to walk with Galleos and the young men. He didn't wait for a response, and Anthia suppressed her delight at not having to give one. She was free for the evening! She knew not to expect her husband until late, as a business meeting in a tavern was sure to include a good deal of drinking beer and telling stories as the various parties got to know each other. Two customers approached, and she stood next to Euippe as they each attended to one. A few moments later the last fish were gone, and the women quickly divided the money and then disassembled the pieces of their fish stall, tucking the support posts, countertop, overhead board, and hooks into a bag that Euippe would wear on her back.

"Until tomorrow," she called to Euippe, and Euippe repeated the phrase as she collected her children. Anthia took Nikias's hand and turned left, walking toward the tentmaking shop.

ALCOHOLIC BEVERAGES

Alcoholic beverages were consumed at all levels of society in the ancient world. They were made from grains such as barley and wheat as well as fruits such as grapes, dates, apples, and pomegranates, and they were often flavored with ingredients such as rose petals, mint, absinthe, and violets. There were known methods of chilling such beverages, including the use of cold water and snow, though they were often consumed warm. Wine was commonly mixed with water, often with three or four parts water to one part wine.

As she walked she wavered in her decision. *Is this wise? Am I risking the honor of my family?* she asked herself again. She wished Eutaxia were with her. *She's always so brave.* She caught a glimpse of the tailor shop ahead where Iarine worked, and suddenly Iarine was outside it, calling her name and running toward her.

"Anthia!" she gasped, stopping in front of her and doubling over, laughing. "I was so excited to see you that I forgot to breathe while I ran over here." Someone bumped against Anthia, stepping on her toes with leather sandals. "Let's go to the shop," Iarine directed. "We're going to get run over out here."

They walked quickly to the tailor shop and stepped inside. "Sit," Iarine said, pointing to a bench. Anthia did, grateful for the chance to get off her feet. The shop was empty except for Iarine's husband, Hero, who was working on what looked to be a *stola*. He held his needle between his fingers and used it to point at Nikias. "He's huge! I obviously haven't seen him for a while, because he's practically grown up while I wasn't looking. Nikias," he added, "you are such a big boy." Nikias smiled proudly, holding tightly to Anthia's leg.

"He is strong," Iarine said wistfully, watching him run and play. "You are blessed. He will be a man someday." Anthia didn't answer as she didn't know how to respond. She knew that Iarine had given birth to three babies, all of whom had been weak and sickly. None had lived beyond the age of two.

"So, you two will come with us tonight," Iarine insisted, breaking the awkward silence.

Anthia hesitated, then offered an excuse. "I don't have any prepared food to share." She held up the bag of roughly ground wheat that she had purchased earlier in the agora.

"That doesn't matter," Iarine said, smiling mischievously. "We have plenty." She picked up a loaf of soft, fresh bread, handing it to

Anthia. "Nikias, you look like a good helper," she stated, gesturing for him to come to her. She plopped a bag of grapes into his hand.

"Be careful with that!" Anthia cautioned, knowing that he did not understand the value of the food item he now carried.

"You can eat a few now," Iarine told him. "They're delicious. I've already had some." Anthia watched as Nikias cautiously picked one up and placed it in his mouth. Her heart felt as if it was breaking. She knew Nikias had never before eaten a grape; they were expensive, and she hadn't ever been able to justify buying them. "They're a treat for us too," Iarine said softly. "Business has been good lately, and I could afford to buy either mutton for tonight or grapes. I chose grapes."

"Done!" declared Hero, setting aside the *stola*. He walked over to the women and picked up an amphora of wine as Iarine choose a small bowl of salt and a bottle of vinegar from an assortment on a shelf. The group left the shop, with Hero locking the door behind them.

They walked silently to the tentmaking shop, Anthia holding tightly to Nikias's hand so that he wouldn't run off. "Ouch, Mommy," he complained. "Too tight." She laughed awkwardly, loosening her grip, and realized once again that she was holding her breath. She inhaled deeply, then exhaled. *I can do this*, she encouraged herself silently.

"How many people will be there tonight?" she asked in as casual of a tone as she could muster.

"Oh, it's hard to say," Iarine responded. "It can vary a great deal. Certainly Priscilla, whom you met earlier, and her husband, Aquila, and Paul. Several of the women who were part of the conversation yesterday in the tentmaking shop will likely be there, some with their husbands and children. There is a Jewish woman named Dorcas who comes with her slaves. Her daughter, son-in-law and granddaughter will probably be there as well."

Anthia nodded. She didn't trust herself to speak. *I feel so unsettled*, she admitted to herself. She walked around a woman who was trying to manage several goats who were bleating and ran straight into the back of a man who was standing and talking in a group with other men.

"Oh! Pardon!" He turned with a smile, and she realized that it was Paul. His smile widened when he recognized her.

"You! . . . Anthia!" he managed after a moment. "And here is Nikias!" Anthia smiled tentatively and glanced at Iarine, who gave her a knowing look. The light from the open door of the tentmaking shop illuminated the faces of the other men in the group, one who Anthia recognized as Priscilla's husband. Paul stooped to her son's level and produced a small wooden horse from a pocket. "Hello, Nikias. I seem to have an extra horse who needs someone to play with him. Would you like to do that?" Nikias stared, open-mouthed, at the toy. It had clearly been carved by someone with skill. He nodded, and Paul held out the toy for Nikias to take. When he did, and then neighed in response, Paul laughed heartily.

He rose and greeted Iarine and Hero, and Anthia watched as they kissed each other on the cheek. *Like families do*, she realized, remembering what Iarine had said yesterday about kin. Priscilla then appeared, waving everyone inside. When she recognized Anthia she scooped her up into a warm hug, and Anthia's eyes filled with tears at the gesture. She blinked them back as she realized why her response had been so emotional. *She reminds me of my mother. She used to hug me like this.* Her mother had died last year after a painful lump in her breast had grown to a frightening size, and Anthia missed her deeply. Her mother had been a mentor, always guiding Anthia as she grew and teaching her about the realities of life and marriage. She had also protected Anthia, keeping her away from her father's angry fists most of the time. Anthia swallowed, remembering the purple bruises that often dotted her mother's body. After an altercation with her father, her mother would gather Anthia into her arms and hug her. Last year, when her mother's cries finally ended and her breathing stopped, Anthia had picked up her mother's thin frame from the floor of their one-room home and hugged her again. One last time.

After another moment Priscilla released her but then took her arm and walked with her inside the shop. The door to the back room was open, and the two-room space held a surprising number of people. Young children were running back and forth, and Nikias quickly extracted himself from her and joined them. She noticed a small circle of men talking in one corner, and she recognized the Jewish woman named Dorcas sitting on a bench with several other women. Facing them on a separate bench were two older men with white hair and long beards who were wearing togas. Several small clay lamps were lit throughout the room, their small wicks jumping in the breeze, and in one corner two braziers were sitting next to each other, emitting both light and the delicious smell of cooking meat. Women scurried around the area, arranging food and dishes, and Anthia noted the *stola*s on some of the women. When Hero and Iarine headed in their direction, Anthia followed them.

Figure 5.1. A brazier, an ancient portable cooking appliance

"Where should we put everything?" Iarine asked an older woman whose *stola* marked her as a Roman citizen.

"There. Near the cushions." She pointed with one hand while holding a child on her hip with the other. "We're about to start." Anthia's stomach rumbled as she looked at the food placed on the floor or on small tables set around the room. There were several cushions and also a few stools. She wondered how the seating arrangements were made. *Will I be in the back room?* she wondered. *I hope I can sit near Iarine.*

Paul's laughter interrupted her thoughts. *His laugh is so recognizable,* she reflected. She watched him walk to the center of the room, where he extended his arms as if he were about to hug a friend.

"Brothers! Sisters! Welcome. Grace and peace to all of you."

HONOR AND SHAME

In the predominantly collectivist cultures of the first-century Roman Empire, key social values included honor and shame. The primary goal in life was honor, which involved *public* (as opposed to private) recognition of status. Honor was often achieved and maintained through wealth, especially if that wealth was used for the good of the whole group (or guild or city), though people on the lower end of the financial ladder could also be honorable. An individual's honor was tied to the honor of the larger group, and either aspect could affect the other. For example, an individual who acted appropriately in light of social norms and was given honor would thus be seen to increase the honor of the group, while behavior that was considered shameful would lower the status not just of that person but of the corporate entity as well.

There it is again. She surveyed the room, again noticing the clothing of the participants. *Let's see who the "brothers and sisters" are.*

Quite a mixed group, she concluded after a moment. The range was enormous: bright white togas on some men, and bright red or blue *stola*s on some women. On most people, both men and women, gray or brown tunics were the norm. *There are high-ranking Roman citizens here, socializing with those of us who are not citizens and rank much further down.* She had seen enough of Paul to know that he seemed to enjoy intentionally flouting the social norm, but this was extreme. The Roman citizens were inviting the degradation of their honor by attending this gathering.

She suddenly realized that she wasn't listening, and she brought her attention back to what Paul was saying.

" . . . why we gather on Sunday. Jesus' resurrection on Sunday indicates the beginning of the true creator god's work in the world to restore what has been broken. Resurrection life has conquered death, and there are many witnesses who can confirm this truth, including the twelve disciples, Jesus' own brother James, more than five hundred brothers and sisters, all of the apostles, and myself. And so we gather to remember and celebrate that hope." Paul bent to retrieve a loaf of bread and a ceramic cup of wine from the ground. "On the night of Jesus' betrayal, he took bread, gave thanks, broke it, and said, 'This is my body. It's for you. Do this to remember me.' After he ate with his disciples he took the cup and said, 'This cup is the new covenant in my blood. Do this to remember me.' Every time you eat the bread and drink from the cup, you announce to everyone the death of Jesus until he appears again and we see him face to face." Paul exhaled loudly, and Anthia noticed the tears streaming down his face. She was shocked by this public display of emotion.

How shameful. But . . . he really believes that. It moves him.
Anthia watched as he attempted to speak through his emotion
but was unable to. He gestured toward Priscilla with his hand,
and she quickly stepped forward with a smile.

"Brothers and sisters, let's eat together as Jesus taught us and remember him well. Let's celebrate and give thanks, for we are blessed
to be part of the community of the true god's restored people!" After
her announcement Priscilla picked up a tray of sausages, while
Aquila hoisted an amphora of wine. The two of them started making
their way around the room, offering the food and drink.

They're serving, Anthia realized. *They're serving, while slaves sit
and eat.* Anthia glanced around, suddenly realizing that she
didn't know where to sit. She stood woodenly, unsure of where
she belonged. *Surely in the back room.* But then Iarine grabbed
her arm and led her over to where Dorcas was sitting, and Hero
followed them.

"I've been wanting to meet you since you walked in." Dorcas
smiled and patted the seat next to her on the bench. "Please, eat
with me." Anthia hesitated, wondering whether this was some
kind of test. Was she really supposed to eat with a Roman
citizen? "Please, sister." Dorcas patted again. Anthia sat, eyeing
the rest of the room to see whether she was in line. Her astonishment only grew as she realized that all of the smaller groups
were mixed. Some were sitting on the floor, and a few had
cushions. A few were on stools or benches, but there seemed to
be no specific organization to the arrangements.

Her expression must have relayed her confusion, because
Dorcas addressed the issue. "We choose to eat the way Jesus ate,"
she said simply. "He ate with those of higher and lower status
than himself. If we follow him in that way, we are declaring with
our lives that we believe he is the one who brings the age to
come, where all are brothers and sisters."

"The age to come?" Anthia asked.

"It is the time of restoration, of resurrection life conquering death, of all things being the way the true god intends them to be. Jesus started it." Dorcas smiled. "Sausage? Pork belly? Grapes? What would you like first?"

.   .   .

Anthia chewed quietly, savoring the pork in her mouth and listening to the spirited conversation around her. She had learned that the young women sitting on the other side of Dorcas were her slaves—her slaves! She had never heard of a master and slave sharing the same bench while dining. A young man named Onesiphorus was sitting on the floor across from them, and an older man named Sosthenes was sitting next to Hero. The conversation alternated between the people in their haphazard circle and then between their circle and those sitting next to them on all sides. It was a raucous experience, but the mood was warm. Anthia had been part of what could only be described as a mob in the stadium when they cheered on gladiators, and that was raucous as well, but the mood then felt dangerous, not safe. She watched Nikias run with his new friends to the back room, each with a sausage in hand, and smiled. She suddenly realized that she needed to use the latrine. *It comes on like a bolt of lightning*, she thought good-humoredly, patting her belly, but when she stood she felt the blood run down her leg. She sat again quickly, pretending to feel faint. The women in the circle quickly surrounded her, bringing water and asking how she felt. Her eyes met Iarine's, and her friend shook her head slightly in acknowledgment.

"I will take her outside for some fresh air," she declared, grabbing Anthia's arm and escorting her as quickly as she could to the door. Outside, the women sat and leaned against the wall of the shop, breathing in the cooler night air. "Tell me." Iarine's words were filled with concern.

"I haven't felt the baby all day. And when I stood, I could feel the blood running down my leg. I don't know what to do."

"May we pray for you? I can gather some of the women together. Jesus is the one with the power to stop your bleeding and help your baby kick. Jesus is the one who can keep us safe during our pregnancies and deliveries and give strength to our babies. It is Jesus."

Not Artemis. Anthia filled in the implied contrast silently, weighing the claim. Her fear was real, for she did not want to anger the goddess, but her desperation won the argument. She thought of Euxinus, running and playing in the street with Nikias. "Okay," she agreed. At her assent, Iarine rose and went inside. Anthia went to use the latrine, and Iarine returned a few minutes later with several women, including Dorcas and her slave Rhoda. The women all looked at her questioningly, and Iarine confided in them.

"We must pray!" Rhoda exclaimed, and the women moved as one to surround Anthia. They placed their hands on her—mostly on her belly—and prayed. Each spoke briefly, imploring Jesus to stop her bleeding and heal her and her baby. Anthia found herself surprisingly moved and attempted to stay the emotion she felt rising in the back of her throat and eyes. *Don't cry, don't cry*, she told herself, willing it to be so.

When it was over the women agreed that they would continue to pray for her, and then one by one they went back inside. Soon it was just Iarine and Anthia. Composing herself, Anthia finally asked a question she had been pondering for a while. "When will we see Jesus? Will we?"

"When he appears again here, in his resurrection body. We don't know exactly when it will be."

"And this time is also when his followers receive their new bodies? What age will those bodies be? Young? Old?"

"Yes, when he is here in his resurrection body, his followers will have theirs. I don't know what age they will be, but I do know that they will be both like and unlike the bodies we have now. It's a mystery."

Anthia considered that for a moment, then asked another question, though she was pretty sure she already knew the answer. "There were women wearing *stola*s who were preparing and arranging the food. Why would Roman citizens serve the food? And then Priscilla and Aquila were serving both food and wine . . . aren't there slaves or lower-status people who should be in charge of that?"

Iarine smiled. "The meal, including the sharing of the bread and cup, is the center of our gathering, and women of all status levels organize it. Sometimes I contribute, and sometimes Dorcas does. Sometimes Rhoda does, but not always. The men often assist as well."

Anthia's shocked look must have been clear, because Iarine continued. "Jesus helped serve food, and he taught his male disciples to do so as well. Dorcas, for example, insists both on serving alongside slaves and that the men help."

"Dorcas and Sosthenes seem to be good friends. But I heard someone mention that he is from Corinth, so how can that be?"

"He is from Corinth but has been here awhile with Paul. Sosthenes is Jewish, like Dorcas, so they share that. They both love the Jewish scriptures and often read them aloud for us when we gather."

"So they can read?"

"Yes. So can a few others, including Paul, Priscilla, and Aquila." She studied Anthia's face. "When we gather, everyone contributes. Some sing a psalm—there are many that are part of the Jewish scriptures—or a hymn about Jesus. They often teach us so we can all sing together. Others teach a lesson or share something that Jesus has revealed to them. Some have a gift from god's spirit to speak in another tongue or language, and others give insight into what was said by the tongue speaker in Greek for the rest of us. Or they might lead a prayer or testify about something that Jesus has done in their lives. And there are more ways that everyone contributes."

"So . . . Dorcas may read scripture, and immediately after that her slave Rhoda might pray?"

"Yes. Everyone gets a turn. Slave or free, Jew or non-Jew, male or female, Roman citizen or not . . . none of those realities exclude anyone from sharing here. The same spirit of god indwells all of us and has given each one of us a gift, at least one. The only condition is that the gift you share must be useful for everyone and build up, encourage, or challenge the whole *ekklesia*, the whole assembly." She paused and smiled at Anthia. "I hope you don't mind me going on so long, but it seems like you're curious."

"No, please, continue." Anthia waved her on.

"There are two main reasons why we call ourselves an assembly: The first is that in the Jewish scriptures the gathered community of the true god's people is called an assembly. The second is that everyone knows how local Greek assemblies work. Only citizens can participate. Here, in this assembly, we are all citizens of heaven; we embody the culture and values of heaven in our gathering. That's why we eat together first, because some in the group are hungry. It may be their first meal today, and in heaven no one is hungry. And then we share our gifts and discuss together."

As if on cue, Priscilla stuck her head out the door and waved them in. They stood, and Anthia waited for the rush of blood down her leg, but there was nothing. She said a silent prayer of thanks to Jesus and followed her friend inside.

■ ■ ■

Anthia sat with the group in a large, messy circle, marveling again at the order within the chaos. The young children sat with parents but then also got up and moved around, playing with only an occasional shriek. The order of the circle was consonant with the meal; there was no order, and people sat in random places, a Roman citizen next to a slave, and a Jew next to a non-Jew. She had expected Paul to speak first, and longest, but the reality was different. Dorcas was first, reading a passage from a Jewish scripture called Deuteronomy. Then a man who called himself Epaenetus said that he wanted to testify to the grace of Jesus in his life. "I have been called out of the darkness of sorcery and into the light," he declared. "I still have my sorcery books. I wanted to sell them, but I feel that the spirit of god is telling me to burn them."

The room was electric as its occupants grasped the weight of Epaenetus's words. Finally, Paul spoke in a quiet voice. "Epaenetus, you were the first to join the Way in the province of Asia. You took that risk, and it seems that Jesus wants you to take another. We are with you."

Burn his sorcery books? Anthia was astounded. *Why must he do that? Why couldn't he keep them, or sell them, or . . .* Her mind was racing, but then Priscilla spoke up and answered her questions. "Dorcas just read from Deuteronomy, and in that same scripture the true god tells us that only he is the lord of all. Only him. That means that we cannot split our loyalty between him and other gods or powers." She turned to Epaenetus. "Burning your books would be a clear indication of where your loyalty lies."

"Tomorrow, then," Epaenetus affirmed. "I will do it near the agora so that any and all may witness it."

Anthia's heart was pounding in fear. *So public . . . everyone will know. So risky. What will happen to him, and to anyone associated with him, at this public shaming of Epaenetus's old gods?*

Her thoughts were interrupted by Rhoda, who told the group about a vision that she had been given by Jesus. She had seen a stream that expanded into a large river as smaller streams and tributaries joined it. She laughed joyfully. "We are a tributary, and we have joined the river of the true god's people." Then a man who called himself Gaius across the circle suggested singing a hymn about Jesus, and others added their voices as he sang.

Anthia listened carefully. The hymn's lyrics were describing Jesus' equality with god, but they also affirmed that Jesus did not exploit this equality. Instead, he took the form of a slave. *Who would do that willingly? Become a slave?*

Next a young woman named Secunda shared, calmly telling the group that they would be tested in their faith, but the spirit of god would be with them. "We must go through many hardships to enter the kingdom of god," she added.

Anthia felt like her heart had stopped. *That's my fear. That being part of this, following this Jesus, will cost me something because I will have shamed myself and those connected to me.* She looked around the circle, trying to gauge the level of fear in others, and suddenly she sensed another presence in the room. *It's like a heavy blanket, warm and cozy. And . . . my skin is tingling.* As she pondered possible explanations for what she was experiencing, a deep calm settled over her, and suddenly she was crying.

Priscilla spoke next, calling Secunda's words a prophecy that must be weighed. Several others in the room then met to confer while a curly-haired man named Aristarchus led another song about Jesus, but this time Jesus was described not as a slave but as the one through whom all things were created, including thrones, powers, rulers, and authorities. Following the song the smaller group who had been weighing the prophecy shared, indicating that the spirit of god had revealed that Secunda had heard her prophetic word clearly and well; it was indeed from god.

A young man to her left cleared his throat, and the group turned to look at him. "My name is Timothy," he began, "in case there are some here who are not yet my friends." At that, he turned and smiled warmly at Anthia, and she couldn't help but return the smile as she dabbed at her eyes. *Stop crying*, she instructed herself silently. "Erastus and I sense the spirit leading us to invite discussion on the text from Deuteronomy read by Dorcas." He now turned his smile on Dorcas, who also responded in kind. "Perhaps you could read it again, Dorcas, then those of us who have grown up hearing Deuteronomy in the synagogue could share what we have been taught, and then we could give time for questions." The group murmured their assent, and Dorcas unrolled the scroll once again and began to read.

Anthia watched it all, pondering with awe the various contributions by individuals, but especially the way in which the larger group received each person's offering. *There is really a place for everyone.*

After the questions were answered to the satisfaction of all, Priscilla asked the group whether there was anyone else who would like to participate. When no one spoke up, Priscilla prayed a short prayer, after which people stood. Some left immediately, while others chatted in small groups or collected their children. Anthia knew that Nikias needed to go to bed, but her question was urgent. She waited while Iarine finished talking with Dorcas, and then she asked her question. "Did you feel the . . . presence? The warmth?"

Iarine smiled and nodded. "Is that why you were crying?"

Stunned, Anthia stuttered. "Y-yes. How did you know?"

"When the spirit moves, people respond in different ways. Some cry."

"Iarine!" A male voice called from across the room, interrupting them.

"Go," Anthia said, gesturing toward the man. "We'll talk more later." She walked to the back room to look for Nikias and found him seated on a bedmat. *Perhaps Paul's bedmat?* She wondered idly, noting the chamber pot and other items that announced the space as a home. *Or maybe Priscilla and Aquila's.* Nikias was playing some kind of game with a few other children that involved sticks, rocks, and his new wooden horse, and he screamed in protest when she told him it was time to leave.

Just then another young woman joined her and told one of Nikias's playmates that it was time to go home. The woman was wearing a beautiful red *stola*, and Anthia recognized her as one of the women who had been organizing the meal. Anthia found herself unsure of whether she should talk. The woman touched her arm, and when Anthia turned, she said simply, "I'm Claudia. I was hoping we would get a chance to talk. I noticed that your son looks to be about the same age as mine. Is he three years old?"

"Almost," Anthia whispered, gathering her courage and continuing in a louder voice. "But he is big for his age. I am grateful that he is strong and healthy."

Claudia nodded her assent before adding, "They seem to be fast friends. Perhaps they could play together again soon, before another seven days have passed." She thought for a moment. "Tomorrow afternoon?" She smiled hopefully. "We live in one of the terraced apartments near the agora. Will you come?"

Anthia knew exactly which homes Claudia was referencing; they were among the most expensive in all of Ephesus. Claudia clearly did not need to work from dawn to dusk to provide food for her family. She forced herself to smile, but answered honestly. "I will be selling fish tomorrow afternoon in the agora, and Nikias will be with me there." Claudia's eyes registered understanding first, and then shame. "Of course, of course. Perhaps . . . perhaps I could come to the agora tomorrow afternoon with my son and find you? I need fish for dinner, and the boys can play. And then . . . perhaps . . . some night after the sun sets, you will join us for dinner?"

Anthia was moved by this obvious attempt to accommodate her rhythm of daily life, as she suspected that Claudia had never purchased her own food in the agora. This necessary activity was almost certainly performed by slaves in her household. "That sounds nice. Our fish stall is almost always set up near the tailor shop where Iarine and Hero work."

Claudia picked up her son and smiled. "Tomorrow, then."

■　■　■

Anthia walked slowly, matching her pace to her son's tired footsteps. In one hand she carried some leftover bread and sausage, while the other clutched tightly to Nikias's hand. Her mind was reeling, and she was having difficulty absorbing and sorting through what she had just experienced. She passed an inscription that, even though she could not read, she knew and understood. It was that important, that famous. It declared Ephesus to be "the first and greatest metropolis in Asia." Her mind flicked again to Artemis, one of the main reasons that Ephesus could call itself so great a metropolis. *Artemis . . . Jesus . . .*

Day 6, Monday

DAY OF LUNA/SELENE

⋅◇⋅

ANTHIA WAS DREAMING. She and Dorema were outside the city, picking mushrooms, berries, and nuts wherever they could find them among the trees and other vegetation. Their children were running, playing, and laughing. Dorema was holding up a beautiful red berry. But when she placed it on her tongue the berry exploded, and a dark red liquid started dripping out of her mouth and onto her tunic. It moved down her body and covered her pelvis, soaking through the rough fabric. The fabric then began to expand, and soon Anthia could see the shape of her friend's pregnant belly underneath it. Dorema watched wordlessly, her eyes wide in horror. She reached out a hand to Anthia, her eyes pleading for help. Anthia tried to touch her, but she couldn't move. Suddenly, she was standing over the simple tombstone that marked Dorema's final resting place. And then someone was screaming.

Anthia awoke with a start, a scream on her lips. Her eyes fell on Nikias, who was sitting next to the leftovers from last night—or what now remained of them. He smiled broadly at her, his mouth full of food. She took a quick breath and returned his smile, grateful for the food that he was now eating. She glanced down at her husband, then around the room to where everyone else lay, but they were all still sleeping. She had no idea when Philetus had returned last night, because she had actually *slept*. Deeply, restfully. Until that dream. *I didn't even wake up to use the chamber pot.* The realization was forceful, and her shock caused her to ponder why she had slept so well this late in her pregnancy. She had felt so . . . she searched for the right word. *Peaceful . . . but now I need the chamber pot.*

As she stood to collect it Nikias realized what she was doing and gestured wildly, indicating his need to go first. Amused, she allowed him to do so, and as she waited she thought she heard someone say "Jesus" through the thin wall that separated their room from Eutaxia's home next door. She focused, listening closely. *Yes, there it is again.* As she stood she noted with relief that there was no blood on her clothing or in the chamber pot. She placed her hand on her belly and recalled the prayers of the women at the gathering of the Way yesterday, and suddenly she felt a powerful kick. *Hello, my son!* She answered, smiling in wonder. *Could it be? Did this Jesus heal me?*

She walked over to Nikias and picked up a piece of sausage for herself, then gestured to Nikias to accompany her. The two of them walked quickly next door.

■　■　■

Just as she was about to knock, the door opened and Lampo's cousin Perilaus and his family rushed out. Anthia offered a hurried greeting and stepped through the doorway. Eutaxia looked up, worry written on her face. Lampo was there as well, though he was clearly getting ready to leave. Euxinus squealed with delight upon seeing Nikias, who rushed to show his cousin his new wooden horse.

"What is it?" Anthia half whispered. "Not Euxinus?"

"Oh no, he's fine." Lampo smiled tightly. "Did you hear about what happened yesterday afternoon, just before sunset? With the Jews who were trying to cast out dark spirits from those who are possessed?"

Anthia shook her head, knowing why she had missed the news.

"Some sons of a Jewish priest were using the name of Jesus as they attempted to cast out spirits. You can understand their logic in a way; the name of Jesus has clearly proven to be powerful, and they wanted to harness that power for themselves. Apparently, instead of asking the spirit's name, they commanded the spirit to come out 'in the name of the Jesus whom Paul preaches.'" Lampo paused, shaking his head, and Anthia couldn't help but flinch. Lampo looked at her and laughed sharply. "Yes, exactly. It didn't go well. The spirit answered by asking their names instead of the other way around. How ironic. His question was, 'Jesus I know, and Paul too, but who are you?'" Lampo laughed again, this time with more enjoyment. "Then the man with the spirit jumped on the brothers, overpowered them, and beat them until they were bleeding. Oh, and he tore their clothes off, so they ran out of the house naked. So . . . you could say that they were cast out by the spirit."

Astonished, Anthia didn't respond immediately. "I don't know what to say," was all she could muster even after a moment.

"Yes. I know. Those watching it near the agora quickly told everyone they saw, and by now I'm guessing the entire city knows. People are afraid. They realize the power of the name of Jesus, that they can't use it for their own ends. Jesus seems to demand a different kind of honor. I don't fully understand it, because what those Jews did makes sense. Of course if you're an exorcist you use whatever words and names you know that have power, especially a power higher than the spirit that you're trying to control. That's how magical formulas work. The gods expect us to do that . . . don't they? But then . . . they were attempting to act as representatives of Jesus by using his name, and perhaps Jesus didn't like that because if they don't worship him they can't be his representatives." He studied her face. "What do you think?"

Anthia glanced at Eutaxia, who looked as if she had already had this conversation. *She probably has*, Anthia realized. *They've probably been talking about this since last night.*

"I don't know," she said softly. She really didn't. Of course, Ephesus was a center for magic. Their "Ephesian Writings"— magical incantations or terms that were inscribed on Artemis's statue and that people could speak or have written on amulets, rings, or bracelets—were famous throughout the world.

They sat in silence until once again Lampo broke it. "And now . . . something's brewing near the agora."

"What is it?"

"Perilaus was out late last night with his association of fish salters—they meet in a shop near the slave market—and he heard some of them talking about a burning of sorcery scrolls today. Then later that evening they were at a tavern nearby and heard even more rumors from the silversmiths who make statues of Artemis. No one's very happy."

The memory of Epaenetus's declaration last night at the gathering of the Way flooded Anthia's mind. The reason for their unhappiness was clear. *This is a public challenge to—a public shaming of—the powers . . . magic . . . the gods. Can this end well for the rest of us?* "Who's burning them?" Anthia asked simply.

"Some members of the Way, the ones who have given their allegiance to Jesus." Lampo shook his head. "Sorcery scrolls are very valuable. Though . . ." he hesitated. "The power of Jesus healed my son. My line will continue because of that. But why must it be as these followers of Jesus insist? Why does Jesus demand complete loyalty? Can't he share his followers with other lords and gods and powers? Why must we choose between him and the rest? I'm going to the agora. I'm not sure what I'm going to do, but I need to see it. Perilaus has already been there and back this morning, and he confirmed that the crowd is growing."

Just then Philetus stuck his head through the open doorway. "I'm going fishing. Lampo, let's walk to the agora together." Anthia could see her father standing behind her husband, who then stepped outside and walked down the stairs with Lampo. The others in the room were busy eating or using the chamber pot.

Anthia knew that she had food to prepare if they hoped to have a second meal later on in the day. She thought of the small bag of flour next door and estimated how much time she would need to make bread or porridge with it. She also needed to empty the chamber pot and collect water from the fountain. She glanced at Eutaxia, whose expression was clear. Her friend stood and handed her a cup of water.

"Let's go," Eutaxia declared, grabbing Euxinus's hand.

■ ■ ■

As the women walked, Eutaxia peppered Anthia with questions about the previous day. "So you found a way to visit the gathering. How did you do that? And how was it? What happened? How do they honor and worship Jesus? What kind of people were there? Was there anyone of high status? Any Roman citizens?"

Anthia responded with careful answers, answering only in vague generalities.

Eutaxia was clearly unhappy. "But . . . did you recognize anyone? And what did they talk about? Who sat next to you during dinner?"

Anthia saw the crowd up ahead. "I'll tell you more, I promise. But it needs to wait until after this." She pointed, and even Eutaxia gaped at the massive crowd that had gathered. Some gawkers were sitting on animals and standing on stools, tables, and roofs in the attempt to get a better view. Anthia could sense the fear among those watching. *It's almost palpable.* Those watching were strangely silent, and the reason became clear as they neared the edge.

Figure 6.1. A street in Ephesus

The people with scrolls up front are talking, Anthia realized. "I need to see," she told Eutaxia, who nodded her agreement. They skirted the edge of the group and walked along the far side until they were near the front. Anthia watched for a gap between bodies, and when she found it, she darted in. Eutaxia followed, and they managed to squeeze between a surprisingly tall man with curly black hair and a short, round man wearing a bright white toga. Anthia searched the faces of those holding scrolls. She recognized Epaenetus quickly. Several of the other faces were also familiar from last night.

" . . . and I confess that I used to practice magic," a young woman was saying. Her skin was so pale that it was almost translucent. Anthia noted that she did not have any scrolls in front of her. "I visited Epaenetus, a magician." She pointed to the man Anthia had met last night; he was standing in front of a large pile of scrolls. "The magic I practiced involved the power of many gods and goddesses, among them Artemis." She paused. "I hereby revoke my allegiance to Artemis and the others. My allegiance is now with Jesus."

The crowd gasped audibly, but their reaction was cut short by the next person in line, a man with skin the color of charcoal and short white hair. He wore a finely colored tunic, decorated leather sandals, and ornate bracelets on his arms. He held up two scrolls, one in each hand, and stood in front of a large pile of scrolls. "Magic has been my life. But now I divulge my most powerful spell." He set down one scroll, then unrolled the other. His eyes searched the leather before finally resting near the middle. Then he read the spell slowly, clearly, enunciating every word.

The crowd was silent, weighing what they were witnessing. They all knew that the most powerful spells were kept secret, because making them public would strip them of their power. Anthia saw a motion out of the corner of her eye, and when she turned she saw Claudia standing with her son on her hip. Claudia was wiping tears from her cheeks, watching the man up front.

"The greatest power is Jesus. No other power or god is equal to him," the man stated calmly. He then pointed to Claudia before adding, "And my family now honors Jesus alone. With our lives."

The woman after him cradled a large pregnant belly in her thin arms. Her hair reminded Anthia of Phoebe's, as even a headband and pins could not contain it as its curls swirled in the breeze. Her olive skin and dark eyes searched the crowd, and then she turned to face the man on her other side, who spoke. Anthia noted absently that he was shorter than her but built stoutly. *He looks strong.*

"My name is Epaphroditus, and this is Vettia. This is Vettia's fourth pregnancy. None of my sons lived to their naming day, even though we petitioned Artemis for protection and strength and wore amulets inscribed with the magical words of the Ephesian Writings that are also engraved on her statue." He held up two necklaces for the crowd to see, then tossed them unceremoniously on the pile of scrolls near him. "No longer. Now we petition Jesus. He is the true protector."

Anthia felt as if she'd been pierced. She groped for Eutaxia's hand, arm, anything—feeling as if she might faint. Eutaxia responded quickly, supporting her with an arm around the waist. Anthia breathed deeply, controlling each breath while her heart pounded.

Epaenetus stepped forward next, his scrolls in a leather bag over his shoulder. He removed them one by one while he talked, naming the gods in each, along with their powers. Healing. Cursing. The ability to manipulate both spiritual and human forces. After he finished with each scroll, he tossed it onto the ground without care, and each toss extracted gasps of shock from those watching. "I confess that I have created and sold concoctions whose sole purpose was to inflict pain on others," he added. "I have exploited many, and greed for power and money has ruled my life. No more. Jesus is the lord of the world, and his demands require a total life change. Repentance. I must live differently, in ways that show who my lord is."

Epaenetus was the last in the line up front, and when he finished speaking he stooped to open a small clay pot at his feet. Using two small sticks, he scooped up a piece of coal that burned a reddish-orange and dropped it on top of the pile of scrolls. Then another. Then another. Others in the line moved as one, carrying their items to the now-burning pile, watching as it grew bigger, the flames reaching higher and higher.

At first Anthia tried to count the scrolls, but she lost track as more and more were added to the blaze. She had of course heard of book burnings; stories of them were famous across the empire. But this was the first time she was witnessing one, and she found the scene overwhelming.

"So much money," Eutaxia whispered in her ear. "Why accept such a loss, when instead they could have sold the scrolls?"

Anthia looked at the crowd, which continued to grow. *Is the whole city here? It looks like it.* Some of the faces looked shocked, while others appeared angry or worried. She spotted Lampo standing near several other men; the conversation was quite animated. As she watched, one of the men turned so she could see his profile. *Paul!* He was gesturing passionately, and Anthia wondered whether he was repeating some of what he had said last night.

"Mama." Nikias's voice was accompanied by a tug on her arm. She realized that she had been holding tightly to his hand, and he was bored and ready to be done.

"Let's go," she whispered to him, needing some space herself. She touched Eutaxia's shoulder, and the four of them started to wiggle their way through the throng.

. . .

As they emerged from the crowd Nikias shook his hand free of hers and darted over to a wall. He started urinating, and Anthia scolded him. "Nikias! Wait. There is a latrine just around the corner."

"No, Mama! Here!" He said, pointing to a pot. Eutaxia laughed and gently pushed Euxinus in the same direction. "That's one of daddy's urine pots. Please, fill it up." The boys shared the pot, enjoying the intersection of their streams of urine.

"I need the latrine." Anthia's comment was answered quickly by her friend.

"Of course you do. Go ahead; I'll watch the boys for a moment."

Anthia entered the dim space and surveyed her options. *At least it's not that stinky*, she told herself. Dirty water from the public bath next door was used to rinse out the space under the toilet seats. There were a couple of men sitting in one corner who were talking while they were doing their business, and when one of them reached for the cleansing stick Anthia decided that she would sit on the opposite end. An elderly woman was near her, rinsing her hands at the basin. Two young girls, whose fine clothing communicated the wealth of their families, walked in giggling.

Anthia carefully checked for blood. *None.* She sat back in relief, one hand on her belly, and the baby inside her started moving. She could see the ripples of what appeared to be knees and elbows even through the fabric of her tunic. *Yes, baby. Move.* When finished, she stood, adjusted her clothing, and rinsed her hands.

Outside, Eutaxia was watching the boys play with a couple of sticks they had found. Several other young children, a few of them naked, had joined them. Anthia stood next Eutaxia, smiling at their raucous play.

Anthia looked again at Euxinus's little tunic, then noted her son's naked body. "Have any more of your customers indicated that they are finished with clothing, or even smaller pieces of material?" The women had been planning for a while to outfit Nikias, but they hadn't found enough to make a full tunic.

"No," Eutaxia admitted. "But I heard yesterday that there is a new shop across the city that sells used clothing as well as material. Perhaps if Philetus makes another good catch today we could visit the shop later this afternoon or tomorrow morning?"

"I doubt it. Even if there are many fish, Philetus will not want to spend any of the money on clothing for Nikias. He is proud of his son's strong body—including the size of his genitalia—and he thinks that there is no reason to cover it up at this age."

Eutaxia nodded. They'd had this conversation before.

"There you are!" A woman's voice rang out behind them. Before she could even turn, Anthia was enveloped in a hug.

"Claudia!" she finally managed, noting Eutaxia's suspicious face. Claudia was dressed as she had been last night—in a beautifully decorated *stola*, this one a deep blue, and fine leather sandals. Her earrings tinkled as she moved, and her fingers were covered with gold and silver rings, some with gemstones.

"I . . . " she began, her mind scrambling as she tried to decide how to explain to Eutaxia. Thankfully, Claudia took over.

"Anthia and I met last night. I am Claudia, and am grateful to know you as well. This is my son, Strategos, and behind me are Severa and Plancia."

"Ahh . . . last night. I see. I'm Eutaxia." Eutaxia smiled, and it seemed genuine.

Well, at least this satisfies some of her curiosity, Anthia acknowledged. She recognized the two young women behind Claudia as well, since they had been at the gathering of the Way. They were both wearing simple brown tunics, though the material looked new and was clean. One of them carried a baby on her back. *They must be her slaves*, she realized suddenly. *She just introduced her slaves to us.*

"Where is Nikias?"

"There, Mama!" Strategos shouted, and he darted off to join the cadre of children. Claudia turned and nodded at one of the slaves behind her, who walked and stood next to the children.

"We are just heading home now. It will soon be time for the midday meal." She paused. "Please, join us. We'd love to host you as well, Eutaxia."

Eutaxia stared, clearly stunned. Anthia felt a laugh bubbling up from inside but worked hard to stifle it. *Now is not the time*, she told herself. *Don't laugh. Eutaxia is just surprised; she's never been invited to share a meal with someone of Claudia's status before.* Then, as realization set in, she worried, *I hope I didn't look this confused last night.*

As if catching herself, Claudia suddenly changed tacks. "Or, if you need to be in the agora, perhaps we could bring food to you. Or . . ."

Eutaxia finally regained her composure. "Would it be all right if we stopped by a bit later? I need to finish some work, but we would love to come after that."

Anthia noted Eutaxia's omission of the location of her work, since she did the mending at home. *She's curious*, she realized. *She wants to see Claudia's home, eat her food, and get a glimpse of upper-class life.*

Clearly thrilled, Claudia smiled widely. "Yes, of course. That sounds wonderful. I'll leave Severa outside to wait for you. That way you'll know which apartment is ours." She called to the slave near the children, who then commanded her young son to come, and the group departed.

Anthia and Eutaxia watched them go. Anthia waited for her friend to speak.

"Her slaves have better tunics than we do. But she's kind. She's clearly trying to include us in her social circle, though I don't understand why. But I'm curious, so I want to go. I may never see inside one of those terrace homes again." She walked toward the children, and Anthia trailed after her.

■   ■   ■

The women walked up the stairs carefully, balancing their water pots with care. Their young sons carried small water jugs as well. Everyone who was physically able to do so, even the very young, helped. They had already made the trek upstairs once because they needed to fetch containers for water. Then they visited the fountain to fill them.

Anthia entered their one-room home slowly, balancing her water pot on top of her belly. Her aunt walked over to help her, and Anthia saw her father lying on his mat behind her.

"Could you ask Eutaxia if she has a bit of yeast or sour juice that we could use?" Anthia said, and her aunt nodded and quietly walked next door, while Nikias set his water container on the ground and then peered over at his grandfather's still form.

"Grandpa?" Nikias's question went unanswered, and he found entertainment instead in his new wooden horse. Anthia busied herself with preparing the bread dough, and when Eirene returned Anthia worked quietly, wondering how to broach the topic with her aunt.

"If Philetus returns to rest, will you tell him that we will have bread for dinner?" The unspoken part of the sentence hung between the women. *And if he hasn't caught anything, bread will be all there is. One small loaf for the five of us. And possibly for Andrew and Penelope and their sons if they haven't been able to procure other food today.* Her aunt nodded, understanding clear in her eyes. "Tell him I will meet him in the agora at our fish stall.

Eutaxia has asked me to accompany her now to the house of a woman who needs to have some clothes mended," she lied, hoping that her aunt wouldn't ask for any more details. Just then, her father groaned and rolled over. He clutched his stomach, and they could all hear what happened next.

He's soiling himself again. Eirene rushed to his side, kneeling so that she could stroke his head while she murmured words of comfort. She knew there was no point in asking him to use the chamber pot. He did so when he was able. They all knew that her father wasn't sick, at least not specifically so. He was just old. Anthia's mother had been his third wife, as the first had died in childbirth and the second from a fever. He had been fifty-three when he married Anthia's mother, who was fifteen. Suddenly his eyes opened, and Anthia could see the tears on his cheeks.

"I'm sorry, daughter. So sorry."

Her heart breaking, she rushed to him and touched his face. "It's all right, Father. And Nikias and I just carried up some fresh water." She turned to her aunt. "Can you help me undress him? And then you can clean him up, and Nikias and I will find a way to clean his tunic." She knew that he would lie there naked until she returned, but there was nothing she could do about that. They carefully pulled the garment over his head, exposing his thin, frail body. She bundled the tunic into a ball and asked for Nikias to bring her a piece of string. She took his hand and nodded to her aunt, then walked next door.

Eutaxia was mending furiously. When Anthia knocked lightly and walked in, she barely looked up from her work.

"I have so much mending to do. I'm trying to finish a few pieces so that I can save the time I need to visit Claudia. This one is almost done." She was working on a heavy woolen cloak. Euxinus sat next to his mother on the floor, legs crossed, needle and thread in hand. Anthia didn't ask about Perilaus and Sophia;

she knew they were working with their children in the fish salting factory.

"What are you mending, Euxinus?" His mother was training him and gave him only the pieces that he could handle with his small hands and developing ability.

"This." He proudly demonstrated his work, holding up a small linen tunic with a tear the size of his pinky finger.

"Done!" Eutaxia announced, setting down the cloak and her needle.

They walked down the stairs silently, waiting until they were out of range of any listening ears. As they neared the bottom Eutaxia opened her mouth to speak, but stopped suddenly when she stepped into the sun. "What is it?" asked Anthia, halting behind her. Eutaxia didn't speak; she merely moved aside. Her finger pointed into the cesspit for the *insula*, where tenants dumped their chamber pots and other refuse.

A baby. Anthia looked at the naked child, who lay squirming in the muck. "Did someone just leave her here, or did we miss her on our way up?"

"I think someone just exposed her; I wouldn't have missed that before." Eutaxia squinted and shielded her eyes from the sun with her hand. "Look at the afterbirth. She was just born." The baby started to cry, and the soft newborn wail competed with the sounds of people and animals at work all around them. Eutaxia started to walk away, and Anthia followed her. This was a fact of life, after all. Babies were another mouth to feed. And the child was a girl, not a boy, though she looked healthy. Anthia turned for one last look and saw a man in a toga reaching into the pit to retrieve the child. He turned and handed the child to a slave standing behind him. Anthia knew what she was witnessing. He would raise the baby until she was old enough to sell. *I wonder what Priscilla and Paul would think about that, since*

Jews keep and raise all their children. The thought came to her unbidden, and she pushed it away. *It doesn't matter.*

"What's that?" Eutaxia gestured to the bundled tunic in Nikias's hands.

"My father had another accident." She smiled bravely. "Do you think it's possible that Lampo might be able to clean it? We could set aside a fish from the next large catch for your family."

"Hmm . . ." Eutaxia considered the request. "It depends on how busy they are today. They have a couple of new fullering contracts that they need to manage."

"If I could find a place to rinse it first, would that help?"

"Yes. He could probably add it to another customer's clothing if you could rinse it off a little bit first."

"Thank you," she said quietly, as she began a mental list of possible options for where she could rinse the garment. The fountains were out; people used that water for drinking and cooking. Perhaps she could walk down to the harbor and find a space on the shore? There were also some streams outside the city; that would be an option, though it could take a lot of time to get there and back. *Maybe after lunch I can head to the harbor, and then go to the agora. Hmm . . . I should go to the agora first. What if Philetus is waiting? He'll be angry if I make him wait very long. But for Lampo to have time to clean it, I need to get it to him before I go to sell fish . . .*

She was so lost in thought that she was startled when Eutaxia grabbed her arm. "There!" She was pointing to one of the slaves they had met this morning. The young woman Severa was looking at them and smiling. They walked up to her, and she ushered them inside.

As they walked through a high, arched doorway into the first room, Anthia tried not to stare. She had never been in a domestic space that was so beautiful, or so large. The walls were covered with images of the gods, and the floor in the receiving room featured a forest scene. She saw slaves tutoring a couple of young boys next to a fountain in a side room, and several others were spinning and weaving in the next—a space with vaulted ceilings and images of philosophers on the walls. Claudia came rushing down from a staircase, exclaiming her welcome. A man Anthia quickly recognized from the scroll burning that morning descended more slowly behind her, along with another younger man who looked a great deal like Claudia's young son. *Her father-in-law and husband?* she guessed.

"Welcome, welcome!" the older man exclaimed. He held a small dog in his hands that looked to be quite clean, well groomed, and well fed.

They clearly have plenty to eat in this house. Even the dog looks robust. Once glance at Eutaxia confirmed that her friend was thinking the same thing.

"I am Hermogenes. This is my son Megakles. We have already eaten and have some business to attend to." The greeting was brief, but a deep smile crinkled the corners of his eyes. Megakles echoed the greeting, then the two of them left.

"Please, come," Claudia said, ushering the women into a dining room where a long, low table was covered with platters of food. Eutaxia inhaled sharply, and when Claudia turned, a look of concern on her face, she appeared to realize the reason. "I didn't know what you liked," she said quietly. "I hope you'll find something that pleases you. Plancia?" The young woman appeared a few seconds later. "Please fetch the children."

■　■　■

Claudia bent and pushed a low bench away from the table, then sat next to it with her legs crossed. Anthia suspected that Claudia, like most of the elite, often reclined while dining, and

THE TERRACE HOUSES

In the first century some elite families in Ephesus lived in what are now known as the terrace houses, a city block of private residences built on a fairly steep slope (hence the name "terrace") in the prime area near the main market. Each of the residences stood three stories high and was composed of multiple rooms for receiving guests, dining, and sleeping. At least one open courtyard (for light and air) often dominated the central space, and most included indoor fountains as well as kitchens and bathrooms with plumbing facilitated through deep wells and pipes fed by aqueducts. Such pipes also were placed under the floors and behind walls as heating systems.

The homes were richly appointed with colonnades, vaulted ceilings, and tiled floors set in patterns of plants, animals, and mythological characters. The walls—often from floor to ceiling—were decorated with

Figure 6.2. The exterior of part of the famous Ephesian terrace houses, a city block of private residences built on a steep slope in the prime area near the main market

marble, painted frescoes, and glass mosaics with similar themes as on the floors. One of the units boasts paintings of naked male and female slaves offering items such as garlands or fish in postures of (sexualized) welcome. Furnishings included inbuilt stoves, benches, altars, pools, and storage spaces, and in Terrace House 2 archaeologists have also discovered sculptures of stone, bronze, and ivory; jewelry; cooking and dining items; and tools.

Figure 6.3. Inside one of the Ephesian terrace houses. Each was at least three stories high

she wondered whether Claudia was sitting instead because of her awareness that Anthia and Eutaxia always ate in that posture. After they were seated one of the slaves bent to pick up a tray of food, and immediately Claudia leapt to her feet to help. Eutaxia shot Anthia a confused look, and Anthia smiled and mouthed "Later." It would take a while to describe to Eutaxia why slaves and free in the Way ate together and served each other.

After serving, Claudia insisted that Severa and Plancia eat with them, and the women assented.

Anthia looked at her plate, which was full of cheese, dates, olives, lamb, and soft bread. She pulled off another piece of the bread and dipped it into the small bowl of olive oil on the table, sighing in contentment. She took another sip of the wine in her cup—her own cup! Though it was mixed with water, Anthia could taste its richness. She wondered momentarily whether there was a way that she could sneak a few dates and a bit of cheese for her father and aunt. They could really use the nourishment, especially her father. Anthia couldn't remember the last time their family had had access to cheese. She glanced at the platter of fruit sitting on the table and celebrated the dessert that was still to come. *I think I'll have a pomegranate,* she decided.

Eutaxia and Claudia were talking about their families, including the many extended relatives that each had in the area. Unsurprisingly, their circles didn't overlap. Most of Claudia's family were Roman citizens and in every way wealthy and elite. They then began to discuss the fullery business where Lampo worked, along with the mending that Eutaxia did. "Euxinus is getting quite good," Eutaxia boasted.

"We need some mending done from time to time," Claudia offered. "Would you be able to take on any more work?" Eutaxia answered in the affirmative, and the women discussed the location of the fullery while Anthia wondered inwardly at this offer.

Doesn't she have slaves to do the mending? Why would she need to hire that out? Or is she trying to be helpful to Eutaxia?

Her thoughts were interrupted by a direct question from Claudia. "Anthia, I noticed that Nikias was carrying a small bundle of clothing when he arrived. Is that his tunic?"

"Um . . ." Anthia hesitated, wondering how to answer. "No," she finally said. "It's my father's. He soiled his tunic this morning. When we leave here Nikias and I will find a place to rinse it, and then hopefully Eutaxia's husband will be able to launder it for us."

"You can do that here. I insist. We have water pumped in through the aqueduct, as well as drains to carry dirty water away to the sewers. And large basins in the back courtyard! Plancia could do it for you if you like."

"Oh no, thank you. I can do it myself."

"Yes, of course." Claudia's eyes moved between Anthia and Plancia, and Anthia felt a bit sorry for both women.

So many of Claudia's natural ways of doing things, how she's been raised, how she's lived her whole life, she's now trying to change. Of course her impulse would be to offer her slave to work for me . . .

"I will show you the basins," Claudia declared, standing abruptly. Anthia and Plancia followed, and Claudia left them alone in the courtyard, saying that she would be back shortly.

"I'll help you," Plancia asserted. As soon as enough water had filled the small basin, Anthia plunged the garment in.

"It's warm," she said aloud.

"Yes." Plancia answered simply.

Anthia took a deep breath, then asked her question. "How long have you been here, in this house?"

"I was born here. My mother and father were also owned by the family, and Severa is my sister." She paused, anticipating Anthia's unasked question. "Even before Hermogenes became interested in the Way, he was just and kind. He did not mistreat us in any way; we were never beaten or our bodies used for his sexual pleasure. But now it is even better, though it is . . . confusing." She laughed softly. "Learning to eat together is messy."

Claudia returned then, carrying something made of cloth in her hands. "Here," she said, holding it up and shaking it out. "Strategos has been growing so quickly; this is now too small. Please," she said, thrusting it into Anthia's hands. "For Nikias. Take it."

The expense of the gift caught Anthia off-guard. "No, I cannot." She handed it back.

"Yes, please."

"My husband will not like it," Anthia admitted, and this revelation caused Claudia to take a step back and think.

"Will he see this as an act of patronage?"

"Almost certainly."

PATRONAGE

Patronage was a central social and economic system in the ancient Mediterranean world. Patrons were wealthier, higher-status people who sought clients in need of protection and/or financial support. Clients then owed their patrons and responded to this debt by performing services to affirm and increase the patron's honor in public spaces.

Patronage was needed because there was almost no social safety net in the ancient world, and access to loans was limited for much of the population. It also served to reinforce the stratification of the population, keeping clients in a perpetually lower status level. Because the most honorable patrons supported the largest number of clients, the competition for clients could be intense. Such competition also explains why the acceptance of patronage came with a cost for clients, but the refusal of patronage also came with a cost, as refusal was seen to be shameful to the patron.

"Then can you tell him that I have hired Eutaxia to do my mending, and I instructed her to get rid of this old tunic, after which she offered it to you?"

Anthia looked at her suspiciously, then eyed the tunic. It was made of finely woven wool and was dyed a dark gray.

"It is true. I will tell her to get rid of this old tunic." Claudia smiled. "I'll tell her now." And she turned and left, the skirt of her blue *stola* swirling behind her.

"She always has a plan, doesn't she?" Anthia offered.

Plancia laughed loudly in agreement, shaking her head. "I was raised with her. In many ways we have always been like sisters, though of course it was my task to take care of her."

Eutaxia appeared a few moments later, smiling knowingly. The tunic was in her hands. "Well, this old thing needs to be dumped in our cesspit, now doesn't it? Unless we could find another use for it . . ." She tossed it to Anthia. "We need to go now if we want to have time to stop by the fullery before the fish stall." Anthia nodded, and just then Claudia returned, carrying a small cloth bag.

"Here. For your father's wet tunic." Behind her Strategos walked slowly toward the group, his small arms encased around a leather bag that was stuffed full. She gestured to him, then added, "He insisted. He wants his new friends to take the left-overs from lunch."

Tears sprang to Anthia's eyes. *It's an answer to prayer . . . and I didn't even pray for it.* She let Eutaxia lead the way, and as she trailed behind her friend, Claudia placed her arm around Anthia's waist and hugged her again—another one of her generous, enveloping hugs—and then moved to do the same to Eutaxia, who was clearly startled by it.

Outside, the women walked silently. Anthia handed the cloth bag to Nikias, who accepted it proudly, and Eutaxia silently removed the bag of food from Anthia's hands and adjusted it in front of her.

"What's wrong with her?" Eutaxia asked suddenly. "There's something off there. Why would she eat with us and share food with us? And give us clothing and . . . ? Doesn't she have friends who share her status? And her family? Is she bored? Does she have too much time on her hands?"

Anthia cast an exasperated look at her friend. "Eutaxia, stop it! You know it's more than that. I agree that it's overwhelming, but be honorable." To her credit, Eutaxia took the critique well, nodding in response. They walked through their normal gate into the agora and headed into the center of the massive space, weaving between the various people, animals, and portable stalls that were arranged without any apparent order. Most of the ground was dry, packed dirt, though a few patches of green appeared here and there. As they walked, Anthia could hear snatches of the conversations they passed. It seemed as if everyone was discussing the scroll burning.

Anthia walked around a young woman who was carrying infant twins in the sling across her back. The skin of the babies was almost as dark as their short black hair, while the woman's skin was a light olive. Anthia recognized her from the slave market. *She's the wet nurse!* The woman's face was blank, and Anthia mourned silently with her. *She mourns her baby. Her son is gone.*

They neared the fullery, and Lampo was clearly visible inside. Sulpicia was again working near the counter, and she spotted them from a distance, calling their names over the din of the market noise. The mention of his wife's name caused Lampo to stop hanging wet garments up to dry, and he met them outside the space. His eyes searched for his son, and when they found him behind Eutaxia, apparently in good health, his eyebrows raised in question.

"Anthia's father had an . . . episode this morning. His tunic is soiled. It's been rinsed, but perhaps you could launder it?"

Lampo turned to Anthia, who added the promise of a fish from her husband's next big catch. *Even if it means that we go hungry that night*, she told herself silently.

"Yes, fine," Lampo stated. "Where is it?" Anthia took the bag from Nikias and held it out in front of Lampo, who accepted it hesitantly. "Where did you get this bag? Looks expensive."

"From a friend," Eutaxia said, ending the conversation as she ushered the boys and Anthia toward the location of the fish stall. "Should we dress Nikias in his new tunic?" she asked as they walked.

"No, not yet," Anthia cautioned. "I want to see if Philetus is there and what kind of mood he's in first." They rounded a small herd of sheep in a makeshift pen and got their first view of the fish stall. "Uh oh," Anthia couldn't help saying. She could see Philetus sitting in front of the stall, and he didn't look happy. Galleos and his sons were there as well, and one of the sons was carrying a small basket of fish.

"Where have you been?" Philetus insisted, jumping to his feet when he saw them approaching. He marched straight up to her and slapped her across the face, shaking with anger. Anthia's cheek stung, but that was minimal compared to her shame. She knew that Philetus was protecting his honor, his actions a response to a wife who had not fulfilled her social expectations.

Anthia could sense from Eutaxia's body language that she wanted to insert herself into the situation, but she did not do so. She did, however, quietly set the bag of food down before stepping in front of it to block it from view. *Smart*, Anthia thought. *That's the best way to help me right now.*

"I'm so sorry, Philetus. So sorry. Um . . . my father had another accident this morning. His tunic needed to be cleaned." She looked at the ground, not her husband. "What do you want me to do?"

"Sell this fish, and do it now," he ordered. "We caught them over an hour ago. We're heading back out to try a different spot in the harbor."

Finally Eutaxia spoke. "Where is Galleos's wife?"

Philetus turned his glower on her, though he did answer. "Euippe is sick." Then he stalked off, gesturing to Galleos's son to hand over the basket. Anthia took it, and she and Nikias started arranging the fish. Some would hang from hooks, while others would be laid out on the counter. He already knew the system.

"Go, friend," she said to Eutaxia. "Your mending awaits."

"I'll make sure that your father and aunt get some of this food now."

"Thank you."

Eutaxia walked away with Euxinus, and Anthia watched them go. *I wonder what will happen tomorrow!*

Day 7, Tuesday

DAY OF MARS/ARES

◆

THE RAIN CASCADED IN SHEETS across the tiny window opening in their top-floor home. There was nothing to keep the water out, and the result was a continuous spray that covered a section of the room. Several holes in the ceiling were letting water in as well, and Nikias and his cousin Demarchos were busily adjusting small containers on the floor to catch the drips. When a cup or small bowl filled, one of them carried it quickly to one of the larger water jugs and dumped it.

Anthia poured another cup of water, using the only cup not being used to catch water. "Drink," she said, again, to the others.

Figure 7.1. An ancient bowl

The men were gone, of course. One could fish in the rain—some even said it improved the chances of a good catch—and Philetus insisted on trying. Andrew had left with hope that the weather might improve his chances of finding work as a day laborer, perhaps keeping others inside and away from the lines. Penelope sat with her baby in her lap; her aunt was seated on the floor, leaning against the wall, while her father reclined on his bedmat. He struggled to sit in order to accommodate her wishes.

"Would you rather we empty the water jug but fill the chamber pot?" His eyes twinkled. "I'm going to need to use it again soon." Anthia smiled at the return of her father's humor, silently thanking the gods for his strength today. *Or should I thank Jesus?* The suddenness of this thought again caught her by surprise, and she decided to put it out of her head. Her father adjusted his tunic, fresh from the fullery last night.

They sat in the only dry spot big enough to accommodate them and divided the leftover food. *Claudia's leftovers fed us for two meals*, Anthia marveled. The baby inside her kicked and then started squirming and somersaulting. "Look," she directed, holding the fabric of her tunic tightly across her belly. "Watch him move." Her aunt quickly placed a firm hand on Anthia's belly, smiling at the feel of the little life within. Her smile took on a sad edge, and Anthia thought, not for the first time, about the pain of her aunt's life. Barrenness was no woman's dream. She covered her aunt's hand with her own and pushed harder, and the baby responded, the movements rippling across her skin.

Anthia smiled, and the effort brought pain to her face, which cultivated the memory of her husband's slap near the fish stall. *I wish he wouldn't have done it in public*, she thought again. *But that was part of the point, wasn't it. To shame me. To demonstrate publicly that my behavior was inappropriate but that he's handling it. At least he isn't here right now.*

She shivered when she remembered his return home last night. It was dark, and everyone had long since gone to sleep. Philetus had entered, announcing to the room a decent catch that had been sold as part of the new contract established two days prior. He had asked about food, and Anthia had risen to light a lamp and show him the food. If the combination of Claudia's leftovers and the hard, dark bread that she often made was confusing to him, he didn't show it. He only grunted and sat to eat while she returned to the bedmat, massaging her sore hips.

After eating, however, he wasn't yet ready for sleep. He used the chamber pot and then joined her on their small bedmat. His hands found her breasts, large and tender underneath her tunic. He pressed firmly on them, though Anthia's small cry of pain went unnoticed. Roughly, he pulled her tunic over her head, grasping at her body with hands and a mouth that were hungry with desire. At first he pushed her down on her back, but her belly protruded too far. He then lifted her up and directed her head toward his lap.

It didn't matter that there were others in the room. Nikias and the other children slept, thankfully. Their breathing was even. The adults all lay still, so still, but Anthia couldn't hear them breathing. She was almost certain that they were awake, listening. They wouldn't interfere, of course. This was the way marriage worked, and the rights of husbands were clear. Anthia was introduced to this reality at a very young age; she could remember nights similar to this, when she pretended to sleep while her father crawled on top of her mother. She had heard of wives who serviced their husbands not just willingly but with pleasure, because the pleasure was returned. Her mind flicked to Iarine, and she wondered what her marriage bed involved. Was there joy, pleasure? She made a mental note to ask.

At least it was over quickly. Philetus grunted several times, then lay back and slept almost instantly. Anthia waited until she was sure he was asleep, then she reached for her tunic and pulled it on. She carefully massaged the sore places on her body and rolled away from him, on her side. And she slept.

He had risen early and left without saying a word to anyone. It had already been raining then.

So now she sat, eating the remnants from the meal shared with Claudia. Penelope and her father and aunt celebrated again the acquisition of such good food, and they asked more questions about the woman who had shared it with them. They forced Nikias to stand and turn, showcasing his fine new attire for the third time that morning. "What a generous family," her father remarked. "And are you sure that you are not in her debt? Does she expect you to pay her back somehow, or honor her in another way, perhaps by praising her publicly in the marketplace?"

"She does not, Father. She made that very clear."

Her aunt leaned back toward the window, then changed the subject. "The rain is ending. When it's over, Nikias and I will bring the chamber pot downstairs."

There was no food to prepare—that depended on Philetus's catch. Because of the full water jugs there was also no water to fetch. She rose, brushing off her tunic. "Could you keep Nikias until the midday rest? I'm going to go to the agora in case there are fish to sell." Her unspoken comment, that it was unwise to wait here until Philetus came to retrieve her, was obvious to the adults in the room. It would only provoke his anger. Her aunt nodded, and Anthia walked out the door.

. . .

Anthia loved the smell of wet earth, and she inhaled deeply as she walked. *Well, as deeply as I can with this baby taking up all the space*, she thought, a smile playing on her lips. She stopped at a public latrine, then continued her walk. She moved as quickly as possible, avoiding the puddles. Her feet were already dirty, but the rain was adding to the grime. The narrow, windy street was packed with people who had also just come outside after the rain. People were emptying chamber pots, carrying water jugs to the fountain, herding animals, and hauling food and other necessities. Children were everywhere, most of them naked. She skirted a group of old women sitting on the ground outside an *insula* and narrowly avoided the contents of a chamber pot that was being dumped out of an upper-floor window behind her.

As she entered the agora, she noticed a group of men who had congregated in and around a shop. The men were talking animatedly, and while she couldn't hear the conversation, the mood was angry. *The silversmiths*, she realized. *I wonder what the issue is. Did one of them cheat the others in the guild? Or are they having supply problems?* She took a short detour so that she could hear more clearly and soon wished she hadn't. She caught snippets of the conversation now and clearly overheard the names "Jesus" and "Artemis." *It's not just anger. It's fear.* Anthia realized. *They all know exactly what's at stake. They make statues of Artemis, and the well-being of Artemis is tied to ours.*

She walked quickly away, trying to force her mind to think about something else. *Don't worry*, she told herself. She rubbed her belly as she walked, and her baby kicked strongly in response. Seeing the outline of the tailor shop ahead, she craned her neck in an attempt to spot Iarine. *There! She's there!* Picking up her pace a bit more, she practically skipped to the front of the shop. Iarine looked up, surprise written on her face, but it was quickly followed by a smile. The two women hugged, then leaned in conspiratorially.

"How are you and the baby?" Iarine got right to the point.

"Fine. We're fine. He's kicking and squirming continually."

"Oh good. I'm so happy to hear that. You know, Paul asked about you yesterday. He wanted to know what you thought about our gathering and whether you felt welcomed."

"Oh yes. Very welcomed. Honestly, the mix of people felt odd, but . . . warm. Friendly. I've been thinking about it a lot. And then I saw Claudia again yesterday."

"Isn't she wonderful?" Iarine began. "She was the first . . ." Iarine suddenly stopped talking, her face concerned. Iarine was no longer looking at Anthia, but behind her. Anthia turned, and there stood Philetus. He looked angry.

"Philetus, I . . ." Anthia paused. "I am on my way to our stall. You must have caught fish, as I was hoping. I . . ." Anthia trailed off as Philetus strode toward her. He said nothing, but one hand reached out and slapped her quickly across the face. There was such force behind the blow that Anthia stumbled, and Philetus reached out with his other hand and grabbed her by the braided knot at the back of her head, pulling her away from the tailor shop by the hair. She stumbled as she attempted to keep pace with him while walking backward, and he yanked harder in response.

By the time they arrived at the fish stall, Anthia had composed herself. He released her, and she fell at his feet without looking at him, knowing that an emotional display would only shame and anger him further. "I had heard that you've been spending time with Iarine and Hero, and now you've confirmed it." Anthia waited without responding, unsure. "Galleos's wife told him about those two and their involvement with an association that honors Jesus."

There it is, Anthia thought. *That's why he's angry. I haven't been faithful to Philetus and his gods. I have shamed him as a wife. He knows.* Anthia stole a sideways glance toward the fish stall and saw Galleos's smug face. Philetus noticed her movement,

HAIR, BEARDS, AND BARBERS

In public settings most free women in the Greco-Roman world wore their hair long and parted in the middle or combed straight back and pulled away from the face, held either with small hairpins (of metal, bone, or ivory) or a scarf, headband, ribbon, or hairnet. Sometimes the hair was braided and wound around the head or into a knot at the back of the neck or head. Slave women often wore their hair shorter than free women. Slaves routinely worked on hair for higher-status women, who also sometimes wore more complicated hairstyles, including piling it into a mass on the crown. Higher-status men and women sometimes wore wigs (including blond wigs imported from Germany and made with the hair of prisoners of war), used curling tongs, or dyed their hair blond or black, especially to cover grays.

While many Jewish men wore their hair a bit longer and favored beards, Greco-Roman men typically wore their hair short and styled it by combing it straight down with no part, sometimes with the help of oil or grease from animal fat or marrow. While the elite used slaves or in-home barbers (and there is evidence for emperors and other wealthy men shaving every day), those of middle status and class often visited barbershops. As in many contexts today, barbershops in the Greco-Roman world were known both for their gossip and their grooming services (which included the use of iron razors and scissors to trim nails, remove earwax, trim hair from the nose and ears, cut corns and warts, and perform minor surgical procedures). Free men on the lower end of the status and economic spectrum lived with untrimmed hair and un-shaven beards, while some male slaves would have their heads shaved.

however, and rewarded it with a quick slap to her head. Dazed, Anthia looked down.

"Never again," Philetus warned. "Never again will you shame our family, our association, or our protector Artemis. You will not talk with Iarine and Hero again." Then he turned and stalked away.

Anthia knew better than to respond directly, even though a part of her wanted to call after him that it was the power of Jesus that had healed his nephew. She didn't, however—this was about Philetus and his honor, especially in relationship to his fishing guild. This was not about the kindness of Hero and Iarine, or Paul and his healing towel.

She got carefully to her feet and brushed off her hands and tunic. She walked slowly to the stall and began to lay out fish, ignoring the stares of those who had gathered to watch the altercation. She wanted to cry, but she knew it would do more harm than good. Willing herself to be stoic, she fought back the tears and cleared her throat, greeting a customer with a forced smile.

Does he know that I visited the gathering? She pondered. *Or does he just think that I'm friends with people who are part of the Jesus association?* Anthia saw another customer approach out of the corner of her eye and quickly recognized Plancia, one of Claudia's slaves. They haggled quickly over the price of a fish, and then Plancia said quietly, "I saw. I was behind you near the tailor shop. Iarine sent me to check on you. She wants to help."

Anthia forced a smile. "There's nothing to do."

"There's always something. I'll be back." And Plancia was gone.

■　■　■

It was time for the midday rest, and Anthia couldn't wait to lie down. She trudged through the agora, grateful to be alone. Philetus and Galleos had headed off together without a word, probably to a tavern. Suddenly someone touched her arm. She turned, surprised, and Plancia was walking beside her.

"I have news," Plancia said, her eyes forward. "Claudia sent me to tell the others about you, and we are praying. We are meeting tonight to pray. Claudia is hosting." She turned then, looking directly at Anthia. "When we gather this evening, we will also discuss how each free member could honor your husband's fishing guild with their friendship and partnership. For example, Claudia's husband would like to offer Philetus a fishing contract for our household. Aristarchus is a miller, and Dorcas owns both garum factories and fish-salting houses. Secunda's family owns a farm outside the city. All of these brothers and sisters are connected in some way to Hero and Iarine, of course." She shrugged. "There are good possibilities."

Stunned, Anthia didn't respond immediately. *They are attempting to provide me with a way to continue to participate in the gathering.* She almost couldn't believe it. She rubbed her belly absently, walking as she thought. She knew the risks, but she also knew how pleased Philetus would be by such honorable business associations. *It's almost a competition between honor and shame,* she mused. *Great honor may balance the great shame I've caused. And enough honor may even encourage Philetus to allow me to participate in the gatherings, if his honorable business partners also do so. Perhaps . . .* Suddenly, the baby kicked. She kept rubbing, and he kicked again. And again. She stopped then, startling Plancia, who looked at her questioningly. "Yes, there are good possibilities. Yes," she said again, louder now, gathering her courage. She thought once more about her baby and how Jesus had healed him. *Yes, Jesus!* she admitted to herself. "Plancia, if I can, I will be there tonight." Her hand moved to her cheek in a gesture of protection. "It depends on what Philetus is doing, but if he is at the tavern, it may be safe."

Plancia nodded once and walked away. Anthia watched her go for a moment, then turned toward their *insula*.

Epilogue

Anthia held her breath. She knew that she was supposed to be breathing, but she couldn't help it. Her impulse with every contraction was to stop breathing and wait out the pain.

"Breathe." Eutaxia's voice was half command, half encouragement. "You need to breathe."

Anthia nodded in acknowledgement, though she was also annoyed. She found these kinds of comments frustrating even though she knew they were given in her best interest. *I'm doing the best I can!* she thought. Then the contraction passed, and she looked again at the midwife, who smiled encouragingly.

Phoebe walked in from the door, carrying fresh water from the fountain. "Here we are," she said cheerfully. Anthia glared at her, resenting Phoebe's cheerful tone. While grateful for the midwife and her friends, she missed her mother. And Claudia, if she was honest with herself. But Claudia could not dare to visit, as her appearance would raise too much suspicion. Philetus was next door with Lampo, after all.

Several members of the Way had made initial overtures to Philetus's fishing guild, and there were possibilities, but nothing had been contracted yet. Even so, Anthia felt hopeful. She hadn't yet committed to Jesus but had been able to participate in a few gatherings when Philetus's absence made it possible. Her stomach knotted whenever she thought about his reaction if she was discovered, but she felt compelled to go.

Another contraction moved in, and she steeled herself for its duration. She wanted to get up and sit on the birthing chair so she could push, but the midwife kept telling her that it was not yet time.

"Breathe." There was Eutaxia, giving directions again. The midwife sat at her feet on a low stool, occasionally examining her for progress. Then a cool cloth was placed on her forehead, and Anthia covered Eutaxia's hand with her own.

"Thank you," she managed between sharp breaths. She didn't understand how some women could breathe deeply and normally during labor. *It isn't natural!*

The contraction waned, and she relaxed into the pillows on the bedmat. Her mind involuntarily flickered to the first time she had visited the gathering of the Way, when the women had prayed for her baby. They had named Jesus as the one who could keep Anthia safe during pregnancy and childbirth, and then they had prayed to Jesus and asked him for his protection. *Jesus. Not Artemis.* She filled in the implied contrast in her head. *Is that true? Could it be?* Dorema's face suddenly filled her mind, and her grief hit her like a punch. She let out an involuntary groan as she remembered her friend's labor. *Her last breath. I can almost hear it.*

Phoebe's hand patted her shoulder as another contraction began. Too tired to resist, she allowed the gesture, concentrating instead on her attempt to breathe and her jumbled thoughts. *Should I do it? Transfer my loyalty to Jesus and the Way? What about Philetus—his honor and his anger—if he discovers me? What might this cost me?*

Further Reading

SOME OF THE EVENTS IN THIS STORY were inspired by Acts 18–20 and 1 Corinthians 11–14 (it is generally understood that Paul wrote 1 Corinthians from Ephesus).

Here are a few other sources that offer helpful background to the culture and events of our story.

Adams, Edward. *The Earliest Christian Meeting Places: Almost Exclusively Houses?* Library of New Testament Studies 450. London: T&T Clark, 2013.

Bailey, Kenneth E. *Paul Through Mediterranean Eyes: Cultural Studies in 1 Corinthians.* Downers Grove, IL: IVP Academic, 2011.

Bain, Katherine. *Women's Socioeconomic Status and Religious Leadership in Asia Minor in the First Two Centuries C.E.* Minneapolis: Fortress Press, 2014.

Balch, David L., and Annette Weissenrieder, eds. *Contested Spaces: Houses and Temples in Roman Antiquity and the New Testament.* Tübingen: Mohr Siebeck, 2012.

Banks, Robert. *Paul's Idea of Community: The Early House Churches in Their Cultural Setting*, rev. ed. Peabody, MA: Hendrickson, 1994.

Baugh, S. M. "A Foreign World: Ephesus in the First Century." In *Women in the Church: An Interpretation and Application of 1 Timothy 2:9-15*, 25-64. 3rd ed. Edited by Andreas J. Köstenberger and Thomas R. Schreiner. Wheaton, IL: Crossway, 2016.

Blanton, Thomas R., IV, and Raymond Pickett. *Paul and Economics: A Handbook.* Minneapolis: Fortress Press, 2017.

Brinks, C. L. "'Great Is Artemis of the Ephesians': Acts 19:23-41 in Light of Goddess Worship in Ephesus." *The Catholic Biblical Quarterly* 71 (2009): 776-94.

Calpino, Teresa J. *Women, Work and Leadership in Acts.* WUNT 2, 361. Tübingen: Mohr Siebeck, 2014.

Cohick, Lynn H. *Women in the World of the Earliest Christians: Illuminating Ancient Ways of Life.* Grand Rapids: Baker Academic, 2009.

Friesen, Steven J. "Embodied Inequalities: Diet Reconstruction and Christian Origins." In *Stones, Bones, and the Sacred: Essays on Material Culture and Ancient Religion in Honor of Dennis E. Smith,* 9-31. Edited by Alan H. Cadwallader. Early Christianity and its Literature 21. Atlanta: SBL Press, 2016.

———."Poverty in Pauline Studies: Beyond the So-Called New Consensus." *Journal for the Study of the New Testament* 26:3 (2004): 323-61.

Green, Joel B., and Lee Martin McDonald, eds. *The World of the New Testament: Cultural, Social, and Historical Contexts.* Grand Rapids: Baker Academic, 2013.

Harrison, James R., and L. L. Welborn, eds. *The First Urban Churches 3: Ephesus.* Writings from the Greco-Roman World Supplement Series 9. Atlanta: SBL Press, 2018.

Hoag, Gary G. *Wealth in Ancient Ephesus and the First Letter to Timothy: Fresh Insights from Ephesiaca by Xenophon of Ephesus.* Bulletin for Biblical Research Supplement 11. Winona Lake, IN: Eisenbrauns, 2015.

Hubbard, Moyer. "Kept Safe Through Childbearing: Maternal Mortality, Justification by Faith, and the Social Setting of 1 Timothy 2:15." *Journal of the Evangelical Theological Society* 55:4 (December 2012): 743-62.

Hurtado, Larry W. *Destroyer of the Gods: Early Christian Distinctiveness in the Roman World.* Waco, TX: Baylor University Press, 2016.

Immendörfer, Michael. *Ephesians and Artemis: The Cult of the Great Goddess of Ephesus as the Epistle's Context.* WUNT 2, 436. Tübingen: Mohr Siebeck, 2017.

Keener, Craig S. *The IVP Bible Background Commentary: New Testament*. 2nd ed. Downers Grove, IL: IVP Academic, 2014.

Knibbe, Dieter. "Via Sacra Ephesiaca: New Aspects of the Cult of Artemis Ephesia." In *Ephesos Metropolis of Asia: An Interdisciplinary Approach to Its Archaeology, Religion, and Culture*, 141-55. Edited by Helmut Koester. Harvard Theological Studies 41. Cambridge, MA: Harvard University Press, 1995.

Longenecker, Bruce. *Remember the Poor*. Grand Rapids: Eerdmans, 2010.

MacDonald, Margaret Y. *The Power of Children: The Construction of Christian Families in the Greco-Roman World*. Waco, TX: Baylor University Press, 2014.

Marek, Christian, in collaboration with Peter Frei. *In the Land of a Thousand Gods: A History of Asia Minor in the Ancient World*. Translated by Steven Rendall. Princeton, NJ: Princeton University Press, 2016.

Richardson, K. C. *Early Christian Care for the Poor: An Alternative Subsistence Strategy under Roman Imperial Rule*. Matrix: The Bible in Mediterranean Context 11. Eugene, OR: Cascade Books, 2018.

Rogers, Guy MacLean. *The Mysteries of Artemis of Ephesos: Cult, Polis, and Change in the Graeco-Roman World*. New Haven, CT: Yale University Press, 2013.

Rowe, C. Kavin. *World Upside Down: Reading Acts in the Graeco-Roman Age*. Oxford: Oxford University Press, 2010.

Trebilco, Paul. *The Early Christians in Ephesus from Paul to Ignatius*. Grand Rapids: Eerdmans, 2004.

Westfall, Cynthia Long. *Paul and Gender: Reclaiming the Apostle's Vision for Men and Women in Christ*. Grand Rapids: Baker Academic, 2016.

Xenophon of Ephesus. *The Story of Anthia and Habrocomes (An Ephesian Tale or Ephesiaca)*.

Yamauchi, Edwin M., and Marvin R. Wilson, eds. *Dictionary of Daily Life in Biblical and Post-Biblical Antiquity*. 4 vols. Peabody, MA: Hendrickson, 2014–2016.

IMAGE CREDITS

Figure P.1.   Ancient Roman relief carving of a midwife, Wellcome Images / Wikimedia Commons

Figure P.2.   Artemis statue, Museum of Ephesus, photo: Lutz Langer / Wikimedia Commons

Figure 1.1.   Monument set up by fishermen and fishmongers at Ephesos, 50s CE, used courtesy of Philip A. Harland / photo copyright Philip A. Harland 2019

Figure 2.1.   Ostian Insula, photo: Nashvilleneighbor / Wikimedia Commons

Figure 2.2.   The Library of Celsus and the Gate of Mazeus and Mithridates, Ephesus, Turkey, photo: Carole Raddato / Wikimedia Commons

Figure 2.3.   Public toilets, photo: shankar s. / Wikimedia Commons

Figure 3.1.   Artemis temple model, Miniatürk Park, Istanbul, Turkey, photo: Zee Prime / Wikimedia Commons

Figure 3.2.   Roman distaff, the Cesnola Collection, Metropolitan Museum of Art, New York / Wikimedia Commons

Figure 3.3.   Roman loom, photo: Hans Wiengartz / Wikimedia Commons

Figure 3.4.   Ephesus bathhouse, photo: José Luiz / Wikimedia Commons

Figure 4.1.   Ancient Greek theatre in Ephesus, Turkey, photo: Bernard Gagnon / Wikimedia Commons

Figure 4.2.   Perfume bottles, Boscoreale, Italy, photo: Carla Brain / Wikimedia Commons

Figure 5.1.   Casserole and brazier, Stoà of Attalus Museum, photo: Giovanni Dall'Orto / Wikimedia Commons

Other Books in the Series

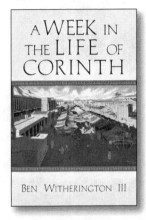

A WEEK IN THE LIFE OF CORINTH

BEN WITHERINGTON III

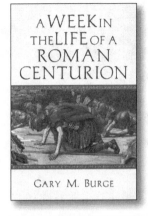

A WEEK IN THE LIFE OF A ROMAN CENTURION

GARY M. BURGE

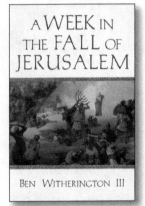

A WEEK IN THE FALL OF JERUSALEM

BEN WITHERINGTON III

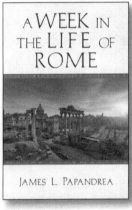

A WEEK IN THE LIFE OF ROME

JAMES L. PAPANDREA

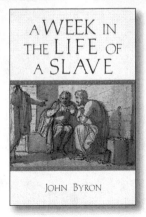

A WEEK IN THE LIFE OF A SLAVE

JOHN BYRON

Finding the Textbook You Need

The IVP Academic Textbook Selector
is an online tool for instantly finding the IVP books
suitable for over 250 courses across 24 disciplines.

---

ivpacademic.com